gets the
Royal
treatment

Jenna McCarthy and
Carolyn Evans

sourcebooks
jabberwocky

Published by Sourcebooks Jabberwocky, an imprint of Sourcebooks, Inc.
P.O. Box 4410, Naperville, Illinois 60567-4410
(630) 961-3900
Fax: (630) 961-2168
www.jabberwockykids.com

Library of Congress Cataloging-in-Publication Data is on file with the publisher.

Source of Production: Versa Press, East Peoria, IL
Date of Production: September 2014
Run Number: 5002369

Printed and bound in the United States of America.
VP 10 9 8 7 6 5 4 3 2 1

Also by Jenna McCarthy
and Carolyn Evans

Maggie Malone and the
Mostly Magical Boots

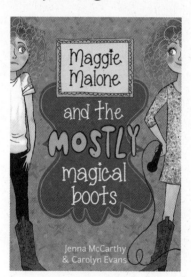

We dedicate this book to Maggie Malone fans everywhere who have been patiently awaiting her next adventure. This one's for you.

Table of Contents

Dear Maggie,

I know you're wondering why I sent you some dirty old cowboy boots for your birthday. Your dad will tell you it's because I'm crazy, but the truth is they were mine when I was your age. I've carried them around the world with me twice, just waiting for your 12th birthday. They might look like a boring pair of boots to you, but trust me when I tell you things aren't always what they seem. These boots will change your life, Maggie. If you let them, that is...

Love,
Auntie Fi

Chapter 1

When I Find Out Princess Apprentices Are an Actual Thing

"So what's the deal with this dance thingy coming up?" I ask Alicia as I slide into my seat in homeroom. I'd noticed a flyer taped to the wall by my locker this morning, something about a Pinkerton Ball and Royal Court Assembly. I have no idea what that even is, but everyone was crowding around that poster like it was a treasure map or something.

"DANCE THINGY?" Alicia shouts, grabbing my hand and squeezing it good and hard. "The Pinkerton Ball and Royal Court Assembly is only THE BIGGEST DEAL of the whole entire school year!"

"A *dance* is the biggest deal of the school year?" I ask. We never had dances at my old school, Sacred Heart.

Instead, the boys got to go on "wilderness retreats" while the girls had these supersized sleepovers in the lunchroom where we wore fuzzy slippers, got mini facials, and slept on air mattresses. I have to say, it was a little bit of heaven—especially the year Beatrice Ballard's mom bought all the fourth grade girls matching pink satin pj's. It was all good times until around 4 a.m. when even the nicest girls went all cuckoo-ca-choo on you from lack of sleep, and the chaperone moms—the same ones who had happily painted flowers on your toes a few hours before— would start to lose it too, going all bushy-haired and bug-eyed just as the sun came up. My mom always thought the whole thing was a really bad idea, and now that I think about it, she may have had a point. Maybe this dance idea is a better one.

"Oh, it's *way* more than a dance," Alicia insists, nodding like one of those bobblehead dolls you see in the back of people's cars.

"Tell us more," Elizabeth whispers, leaning in for the scoop.

Elizabeth showed up at Pinkerton the same week I did and we bonded right away. She's super sweet, but she barely ever speaks above a whisper, so I only get about every third word. I can see her mouth moving really fast and I know she's got a lot to say, but bits and pieces are all we hear. Since Elizabeth's mom talks the same way, we don't expect the volume to get turned up anytime soon. But that's okay. Everybody's got their little thing, right? I mean, I chew the inside of my cheek whenever I talk to a cute boy. The other day when Jake Ritchie said hi to me in the courtyard, I tasted blood for two hours.

"Well, every year, the sixth and seventh grades each elect three princess apprentices," Alicia explains, tucking a stray blond strand behind her ear. "They're going to announce them this Friday during morning assembly!"

"Wait, wait. What the heck is a princess apprentice?" I ask.

"Oh! Well, it's a really big deal to be a princess apprentice because for the whole next year, you get to serve the actual Pinkerton Princess—the eighth grade girl chosen by the school to reign," Alicia explains. "A princess apprentice gets to carry the Pinkerton Princess's book bag, take her lunch order, and bring her towels after PE. It's a huge honor."

"You're serious?" I ask. Alicia nods enthusiastically. I cut my eyes over to Elizabeth to see if she understands the glory of securing a spot on the Pinkerton Royal Court. She smiles, and I get the feeling she might just think the idea is as flat-out wacky as I do. But since we're both pretty new to this school, I figure it's probably best not to poop on the royal parade.

Elizabeth's family moved to town to be closer to her grandparents the same week I had to switch from Sacred Heart to Pinkerton when my dad lost his job. You'd better believe I was not happy about it, especially since I turned twelve about five minutes after I got to Randolph J. Pinkerton Middle School. Twelve was looking pretty lame there for a while, between getting separated from my BFF Stella, getting clobbered with a history book on my very first day of class, and basically finding out I was next to invisible at Pinkerton. But then my crazy Aunt Fiona sent me the Mostly Magical Boots and Frank-the-genie showed up and everything changed.

I know what you're thinking: *Magical boots? A genie named Frank? Yeah, right, Malone. You've been mixing Pop Rocks and Coke again, haven't you?* Trust me, I was right there with you. Especially when Frank-the-genie told me the part about how the boots are *mostly* magical. And then I was all, *if these boots can't make me fly or turn my brother Mickey into a hamster, what good are they?* But it turns out, whenever I put on the Mostly Magical Boots (MMBs for short) and say the magic words—something I did by *accident* the first time, before Frank had a chance to tell me how the MMBs work—I get to be somebody else for a whole day. *Anybody I want.*

Awesome, right?

So now I'm living proof that magical boots and genies are real, because I already spent a day as Becca Starr, the most famous rock star in the universe. I got to ride on her tour bus and get my hair and makeup done and sing onstage for twenty thousand screaming fans. Oh, and I got to meet Justin Crowe, the second most famous rock star in the universe and, it turns out, a super-nice, *totally normal* guy. The only part about the MMBs that stinks is that I can't tell anyone about the boots—not even Stella—or the magic will disappear right off them. *Poof!* Just like that.

Rats, right? *I know.*

"Why is the Royal Court such a big deal?" I ask Alicia now, trying to wrap my brain around the whole idea.

"Well," Alicia gushes, "everyone knows that you can't be a Pinkerton Princess or Prince someday if you never served as a princess apprentice or a duke. Plus…"

"Plus what?" Elizabeth and I ask at the exact same time when she drags out the word for a year and a half.

"Plus, every single year except one, the Marshmallow Queen—which I'm sure you guys know is the highest title at the biggest festival in town—was a former Pinkerton Princess! So the royal court is really a launching pad for *all sorts* of great things."

"If you say so," I tell Alicia. After all, Alicia is practically the mayor of Pinkerton. She knows everyone and is nice to everybody—including the new girl in the ridiculous reindeer sweater. (That was me.) She's been great about showing me the ropes around here, so I guess I'm going to have to believe her when she says this Pinkerton Ball business is all kinds of awesome. Even though, if I'm being honest, it sounds like the silliest thing since canned string.

Chapter 2

When the Meanest Girl at School Gets a Sparkly Pink Tiara

All week long, it's like the only thing anybody can talk or even think about is the Friday assembly. I even heard clumsy Carl Lumberton—he's the guy who dropped the giant text-book on my head that first day—talking about wanting to be a duke. I'm just not seeing that. The day after Carl accidentally knocked me out, he taped this note to my locker:

> Dear new girl,
>
> I'm sorry that I crushed your skull with my history book. That must have really hurt. I hope you don't get a Harry Potter scar from it. There was a lot of blood.
>
> From: Carl

I appreciated knowing that nobody was using my "new kid" head for target practice on purpose, but Carl Lumberton, duke material? Not so much. You see, Carl is kind of a spaz. In my two whole weeks at this school, I've seen him send sporks flying in the lunchroom and school dance flyers sailing down the hall. The poor guy can't seem to hold on to anything for very long— except a football, I hear, so at least that's something.

Finally it's Friday. I love Fridays almost as much as I love my neighbor Mrs. G's cinnamon sticky buns. Everyone is always in a good mood, and the teachers even seem to relax a little. As I cruise up to the bike rack, though, my hopeful good mood starts to sink. Something is going on in front of the school—it looks like a mob or a riot or something. Hundreds—maybe thousands—of students are swarming around outside the multipurpose room, or MPR as it's called here. I lock up my bike and take a deep breath before I start moving toward the crowd. *I hope nobody's gotten hurt*, I think to myself. That's when I hear the chanting.

"All hail our Pinkerton Dukes and Princess Apprentices! All hail our Pinkerton Dukes and Princess Apprentices!"

8

This cannot be for real.

"Hey," whispers Elizabeth, who has snuck up beside me. "What *is* all of this? Is that a *red carpet* going into the MPR?"

The chanting is getting even louder, and Elizabeth and I look at each other and shrug. Just then, an actual trumpet blares—a trumpet!—and the double doors to the MPR fly open. The crowd gets so quiet you could hear a beetle sneeze. My mouth drops to the ground.

Standing in the doorway is Mr. Mooney, the principal of Pinkerton. Normally he wears some version of the same depressing gray suit and brown knit tie. But not today. Today Mr. Mooney is wearing a long crushed velvet robe the color of a ripe raspberry. It's got this thick white fur trim all along the opening in the front and around the cuffs. As if that weren't enough, he's got a huge gold crown studded with different colored jewels on his head and he's carrying one of those fancy wands that kings carry. I'm pretty sure it's called a scepter. Also, I am not positive, but from where I'm standing it looks like he's wearing *makeup*! I try not to laugh, even though I saw that exact outfit in the *Halloween Spooktacular* catalog last year.

"Here ye, hear ye," Mr. Mooney bellows. "I welcome you all to this morning's assembly, where we will be officially announcing this year's Pinkerton Royal Court Assembly! Please enter and take your seats so we can get started." Elizabeth and I exchange stares. *He's talking in a British accent!* Mr. Mooney makes this great sweeping motion with his arms and nearly thwacks the office secretary, Mrs. Dunst, in the head with his scepter. (Some kids call her Mrs. Dunce, but I'm thinking that's only since it rhymes, because she seems smart enough.) With his arms spread out like an overdressed scarecrow, Mr. Mooney drops his chin to his chest and steps backward slowly into the MPR.

"As you all are *very* aware," Mr. Mooney says when everyone finally gets settled, "the Pinkerton Ball and Royal Court Assembly is an esteemed and long-standing tradition here at Randolph J. Pinkerton Middle School. Aside from the actual crowning of the Pinkerton Prince and Princess at the ball next month, the appointing of the royal court—the honored dukes and princess apprentices—is perhaps one of the most significant events of our school year."

I'm practically knocked into next week by the

sound of the entire student body clapping, whistling, and woo-hooing their heads off.

"Without further ado," Mr. Mooney continues, slipping in and out of his terrible fake accent, "let us start with the sixth grade!"

Mrs. Dunst walks onto the stage and hands Mr. Mooney a giant scroll. Man, they think of everything here.

"The first sixth grade princess apprentice will be… drumroll please…"

Mrs. Dunce punches her little CD player and a recorded drumroll plays.

"The one, the only, the *lovely*…Lucy St. Claire!"

Lucy St. Claire. Of course. Lucy—secretly known around Pinkerton as Lucifer—is pretty much the meanest girl I have ever met. (You'd have to be pretty awful for people to call you another name for the *devil*, right?) My very first day at Pinkerton, she made me move out of *her seat*. Apparently, she thinks she owns the place since her grandfather donated some bleachers a hundred years ago. Her family owns a big company that makes the metal part that goes on the top of your pencil to keep your eraser from falling out or something like that. Alicia says the whole school looks forward to her birthday because every year her dad arranges for this amazing carnival to be set up on the football field. Two years ago, Justin Crowe—yes, the super-famous rock star—popped out of her big birthday cake at the end. Alicia said that for some reason Lucy's parents skipped it this year, but nobody knows why. I've tried smiling at Lucy in the hallways, but she usually just glares at me and looks away. Now I mostly try to stay away from her.

I can't see Lucy at first when her name is called, but then I spot her making her way onto the stage as a group of eighth graders tosses rose petals at her feet. I'm thinking she must have been pretty confident about landing an apprentice spot today—she's wearing a strapless black dress and gold high heels. To school! (I'm not allowed to wear anything strapless until I'm fourteen, and I don't think I'll *ever* be able to walk in high heels.) When Lucy reaches Mr. Mooney, he nods at Mrs. Dunst, who fiddles with her CD player again until the famous song from the Miss Galaxy Contest starts to play.

And then—I promise I am not making this up— this beautiful girl I've never seen before steps out of the shadows of the stage wearing a royal blue gown and a sash that says "Marshmallow Queen." She walks up behind Lucy and places a sparkly pink tiara on her head. When she does, Lucy hunches over, looking like she's going to puke or something. Then she stands back up—clutching tight to that crown—and I can see that she is not in fact going to puke but is sobbing her head off. She's shaking and heaving and gasping like she's one of those guests in the studio of the *Helen Show* the day they are giving out brand-new cars to everyone in the audience. She throws her arms around the marshmallow girl, who for some reason is crying too.

"Who's the marshmallow girl?" I whisper to the girl on my other side.

She looks at me like I have worms crawling out of my ears. "Emily Littleton?" she says with that *duh* sound in her voice. "She's only last year's Pinkerton Princess who went on to become the reigning queen of the Marshmallow Festival. She's, like, *legendary* at Franklin High."

"Oh," I say, nodding because I get the feeling I'm supposed to be impressed.

"Can you even *imagine* being her?" the girl sighs.

"Not really," I admit. Because I really, honestly can't.

Chapter 3

When Stella Gives Me a Royally Good Idea

"So how are things over at Stink—at Pinkerton?" Stella asks.

See, before I went to Pinkerton, Stella and I—and everyone at Sacred Heart and pretty much all over the rest of the world as far as I can tell—called my new school Stinkerton. But I decided if I was going to be stuck at this place, I was going to have to give it a chance. And as soon as I made that decision, things really did seem to get better, so I'm trying to stick with that plan.

Anyway, Stella and I like to say we've been friends since "before we were born" because our moms have been best friends since they were our age. Back at Sacred Heart we were inseparable, so much so that most people thought of us as one person named Maggieandstella. If they did use our separate names, half the time they'd get them mixed up—which is funny because Stella and I are polar opposites in the looks department. I have green eyes, pale skin (my mom calls it "peaches and cream," but it's way more cream than peaches), this crazy mess of gold ringlets that look a tiny bit reddish in the sunlight, and freckles across my nose. Stella has chocolate-colored eyes, stick-straight hair so black it's almost blue, and skin the color of caramel candy.

"Actually, things are getting royally ridiculous over there," I tell her.

"Oh yeah?" Stella says, looking up from her laptop. "Tell me more!"

We are flopped out on my zebra rug, scanning the Celebrity Times home page, which is our favorite thing in the world to do besides ride our bikes to Dippin' Donuts and chow down on doughnuts the size of our heads.

"Well, there's this big deal about the Pinkerton Ball and Royal Court Assembly and everybody is going totally nutso about the whole thing," I explain. "It's pretty ridiculous if you ask me."

"Royal Court Assembly?" Stella laughs. "That's hilarious! What does that even *mean*?"

"Well, the sixth and seventh grades each pick three dukes and princess apprentices—stop laughing!—who kind of serve the eighth grade Pinkerton Prince and Princess when they're elected. Like, they get to carry their books and order their lunch and stuff. Seriously, Stella. It's not *that* funny."

Stella is rolling back and forth on my zebra rug, bent legs stomping, making sounds like a spastic hyena. I do love her, but she really can take things a teensy bit too far sometimes.

"I'm sorry, Maggie...I just...I can't...princess... apprentices..." she spits out between spasms. "Princess apprentices!"

"It's not *that* bad," I say, feeling my cheeks begin to burn. "It's actually a real honor to be picked to be an apprentice. They have a prince—and dukes too! Last year, the eighth grade Pinkerton Princess was crowned Marshmallow Queen for the whole county."

"Marshmallow Queen? Seriously, Maggie," Stella says, sitting up. "You're starting to scare me with all this fake, made-up royal talk. You want to talk about princesses? Check *this* out."

Stella slides her laptop my way and points to the Celebrity Times home page.

"Now *here's* a real princess." Stella angles the laptop so we can both get a look at Princess Mimi, the one and only Princess Wilhelmina of Wincastle. She's holding a ribbon next to a beautiful black stallion, probably after one of those big fancy horse shows she's always doing.

Stella and I have been kind of obsessed with Princess Mimi ever since we were eight and *Tween Scene* magazine did a big cover story on her. Mimi had just turned ten at the time, and I guess over in Wincastle that's a major big deal. They had this week-long party for her with about thirteen different cakes, each one the size of a kitchen table. They showed her being escorted into one of the parties by an army of soldiers all dressed in red, and of course she was wearing a real diamond tiara, which Stella and I agreed was the coolest thing ever. It's sort of embarrassing to admit, but until I read that article, I didn't even realize that princesses were *real*. Seriously. I mean I knew they had princesses in the olden days, but I kind of thought they died out like dinosaurs or something and that they were mostly made up for fairy tales and movies. I certainly didn't think there were princesses *my age* out there in the world right this very minute being all royal and everything.

But since I figured that out, Stella and I have spent a lot of time imagining what Princess Mimi's life might be like. We decided she probably sleeps in her tiara and has a solid gold hairbrush and monogrammed toilet paper. (We also designed our own personalized TP, just in case we found out we were princesses. Mine was going to be pink leopard print and have MM on every square; Stella picked turquoise circles with one big aquamarine S in the middle. I tried to argue that turquoise and aquamarine are pretty much the same thing. Didn't she want a little *contrast*? But she wouldn't budge. When Stella gets her mind set on something, there's no use even trying to change it.)

"Jeez," Stella says, skimming the story. "Could Princess Mimi's life *get* any better? She's fourteen and owns an entire *country*. Not to mention a yacht and a plane and a stable full of horses. *And* she's on the cover of a zillion magazines every single month. Can you imagine being called Your Royal Highness for real? 'Oh, did somebody call Her Royal Highness? Yup, that's me, right here!' *Seriously*."

"*And* she has front-row seats at all the fashion shows and gets driven around in a limo," I add, forgetting all about pretend princess apprentices for a minute. We flip through a slideshow with pictures of Princess Mimi lounging on the back of a ship, loaded up with shopping bags, and riding a horse that looks exactly like Black Beauty from the movie.

"I'll bet she never has to do chores or make her own bed," Stella says with a sigh. "She probably even has a royal toothbrusher to do *that* for her."

"She's big-time into volunteering too," I say, because my mom says it's more important to focus on what people do than what they have. "She's always helping to build a school or save a forest or deliver food to someplace you can't pronounce. The only charity work I've ever done is bake oatmeal cookies for our class bake sale that time we were trying to raise money to adopt an acre of rain forest. I don't even know what we *did* with that acre—or even what an acre is!"

"What*ever*," says Stella. "I'm just saying the girl's pretty much got it made. I'd love to have her life."

"Who wouldn't?" I ask.

"Well, at least you've got that princess apprentice thing going on at school," Stella says. "I'm sure it's pretty much the same thing."

"Very funny," I say, giving her a sideways shove that sends her rolling around the floor again—the girl seriously cracks herself up—but I'm hardly paying attention anymore. *Or*, I think to myself, *I could slip into my trusty MMBs and become actual royalty—the one and only Princess Wilhelmina of Wincastle—for a whole entire day.*

"Hey, look at *this*!" I shout, reading the latest royal report on the website. "It says here that Princess Mimi is going to be a bridesmaid in her cousin Princess Clementine's wedding next week."

"What?" Stella says, sitting up to get the scoop. "That's only going to be *the* royal party of the year! And Mimi gets to be right smack in the middle of it. On a scale of one to totally completely not fair, that's like an eleventy billion."

Stella stands up, announcing that she's got to go

home to feed Shrek, her African dwarf frog. That thing is totally lame. All he does is stick to the side of his tank like a fat green "X." He's not much of a pet, but he's all she's allowed to have since she let her hamster Peach go for a swim in the washing machine and then tried to fluff up his fur in the drier.

Rest in peace, Peach.

"Some girls have all the luck," I tell Stella, thinking that maybe I could be one of them. At least for a day.

Chapter 4

When I Get an Offer I'd Really Like to Refuse

The next morning during science, Mrs. Shankshaw is reading from the textbook while we're all blinking like a bunch of deer at a disco and trying to stay awake. Well, most of us are trying to stay awake—some of us, like Carl Lumberton, are sleeping with our mouths wide open, drooling on our desks.

"Cell division takes place in a series of phases or stages…" Mrs. Shankshaw continues in her brain-melting voice, until there is a knock at the door and Mr. Mooney sticks his head in.

Sweet relief! I think. Maybe we can have a fire drill or a school-wide lice screening instead of being forced to listen to the most boring teacher on the planet for another miserable minute.

"I need Duke Lumberton and Lady St. Claire for duke and princess apprentice training, please," Mr. Mooney announces to the class with a smile and a wink. Lucy snaps her book shut, quickly gathers her things, and sails to the front of the class with a big, smug smirk on her face.

I poke Carl in the back. "Mr. Mooney wants you," I whisper. He shoves a notebook, a highlighter, and two pencils off his desk and onto the floor when I do. It takes him forever to collect his stuff, but finally he follows Mr. Mooney and Lucy out of the room.

Seriously? These fake dukes and princesses get sprung out of class for *training*? Alicia says Mr. Mooney is so gung ho about the whole thing because he was a duke back in the day, but apparently he was never elected Pinkerton Prince. All I know is I'd get trained to be a snake handler or an alligator wrangler if I could skip out on this torture.

Since I'm still newish, I don't know any of the other girls, besides Lucy, who were chosen to be princess apprentices, but they're not hard to spot around school. The six of them wear their tiaras all day every day, even during PE. Mr. Walters, the PE teacher, tried to get this one girl to take hers off while we played field hockey—"It's a danger to the rest of the class!" he'd argued—but she threw a hissy fit and threatened to get Mr. Mooney involved so Mr. Walters had let it go. Apparently nobody messes with Mr. Mooney when it comes to anything having to do with the Pinkerton Ball and Royal Court.

Twenty long minutes later, the bell rings and it's lunchtime. I love lunch. Not as much as I loved it back at Sacred Heart with the delicious homemade breads and desserts, but I've got a bagel with cream cheese and jelly on it today and I've been thinking about it all morning. I stop by my locker for my lunch bag and am heading for the lunchroom when Winnie Ipswitch stops me in the hall with a firm tap on the shoulder from behind, which kind of scares the bejeesus out of me. I don't even know what a bejeesus is—that's just something Grandma Flannery says when my little brother Mickey sneaks up on her while she's sewing. My mom says that's a really mean thing to do to an eighty-year-old woman, but Grandma Flannery is from the old country and really tough, my dad says.

"Maggie, Lucy needs to talk to you," Winnie says,

like she's just relayed an urgent message on behalf of the royal apprentice posse.

"Oh, um, okay…" I stammer. "I'm meeting Elizabeth and Alicia for lunch at the picnic tables, so maybe after that?"

"No, *not* after that! She wants to talk to you now!" Winnie insists. "And anyway, Elizabeth and Alicia will be at the meeting too. So let's go." I haven't been around Winnie Ipswitch too much, but she seems like the kind of kid who'd demand twenty dollars' worth of tokens from her mom to try and scoop up a two-dollar stuffed animal with that giant claw thing at the bowling alley. She's obviously used to getting her way, and I'm starting to worry that she might hold her breath (if she could get her lips closed over the top of her bright blue-banded braces) and start stomping her feet until I agree to do what she says.

"Oh, okay, Winnie," I sigh, and take a deep breath.

Elizabeth and Alicia didn't say anything about a meeting with Lucy, but whatever. I'm starving, so I dig in to the dill pickle potato chips in my lunch bag.

I follow Winnie to a small classroom where

Elizabeth and Alicia are sitting at a bunch of desks pushed together, listening closely to Lucy.

"Oh, so glad you could join us, Maggie," Lucy says like she doesn't mean it at all.

Winnie runs over to whisper something into Lucy's ear. "It really doesn't matter, Winnie," Lucy says. "I'm sure Maggie will be glad she's here when I tell her the good news."

Alicia looks over at me with an excited grin and I wonder what she knows.

"I've already explained this to Alicia and Elizabeth, who reported right on time," Lucy says with a nod in their direction. "But I'll go ahead and say it again for your benefit. Next time, though, I'd really appreciate it if you'd come immediately when you're called."

Huh? I think this apprentice business has gone to her already oversized head.

"I've talked it over with Mr. Mooney," Lucy continues, "and he's agreed to let each princess apprentice choose three handmaidens to serve them for the following princess term. Just like the apprentices serve the *actual Pinkerton Princess*, the handmaidens will serve *us*!" Lucy sits back with a wide, generous smile.

"I told Mr. Mooney that it wasn't fair that the princess apprentices should get all the glory—we should *share* that glory—and he agreed it was the right thing to do."

I think I must have actually fallen asleep in Shankshaw's class and I'm the one drooling on a desk dreaming this. Or I have really low blood sugar. My brain does go all wacky when I don't eat. I'll probably start getting dizzy soon—that's what happened right before I passed out at Sacred Heart Field Day last year when I accidentally skipped breakfast *and* lunch.

"Wait," I say, shaking my head, trying to focus. "Did you just say *handmaidens*? Aren't those, like, servants?"

"Well of course they're not *servants*," Lucy says, like she's offended. "Handmaidens are highly regarded helpers with very important duties, I'll have you know. Anyway, as I was *trying* to say…"

"Oh, just tell them!" Winnie blurts out. "It's so exciting!"

"I've chosen *the three of YOU* to be my handmaidens!" she finally comes out with it as Winnie tosses confetti into the air over our heads.

Alicia and Elizabeth beam with joy, hop up from the table, and run over to hug Lucy.

I pick a glittering piece of pink confetti from my lip, give my curls a shake since I know they're a magnet for fluffy flying stuff, and try to make sense of what I've just heard. Before I can stop myself, the only words that my brain can form leap right out of my lips.

"Um, yeah, I'm not really sure about that."

Everybody gasps. Then the room gets quieter than the time the whole Flannery clan had Thanksgiving at our house and three-year-old Mickey came back from the bathroom announcing to the table that he'd made a doodie. With poop all over his hands. You've never seen a table full of Flanneries scatter that fast. The poor kid's never going to live that one down.

Lucy glares at me like a starving, angry wolverine.

"What. Did. You. Just. Say?"

Chapter 5

When I Find Out What It Means to Be Somebody's Handmaiden

"Well, um, I—" I start, but Lucy cuts me right off.

"Who do you think you *are?*" she spits at me. "You're *brand new* at this school, in case you've forgotten that, Maggie Whatever-your-last-name-is. I could have any girl I want to be my handmaiden, any girl in this whole school, and believe me, you were *not* my first choice. You weren't even in my top *one hundred*. You and your other new-girl friend here are nobodies as far as I'm concerned." Elizabeth winces like she just got slapped in the face when she hears this. "But Alicia convinced me that I should give you guys a chance. I can't believe I ever listened to her."

I look at Alicia, whose chlorine-water-blue eyes are

brimming with tears. One blink and they're going to be all over her face. If I don't agree to this hand-maiden business, Lucy is going to make Alicia pay for even suggesting me and Elizabeth. Big-time. Poor Elizabeth looks like she's about to lose it too. Her usually sparkly eyes look like a basset hound's—but way sadder, if that's possible. *Come on, Malone. Say something fast. And make it good.*

"I'm sorry, Lucy," I say.

"You should be," she interrupts, all red-faced and furious.

"No, I'm sorry that I didn't get to finish what I was going to say," I add.

"Oh," Lucy pouts, crossing her arms over her chest. My dad says that when somebody does that, it means they're totally not even planning to give you a chance. "Go on then."

"I think the handmaiden idea is great, really great," I say, scrambling for some way to dig myself—and my new friends—out of this hole.

Lucy smirks, which I think is the closest thing to a smile she's got. Her arms start to relax a little.

"I just think, you know, maybe it's not fair to

Winnie here," I say. *Nice save, Malone.* Auntie Fi always says I'm great at thinking on my feet. I bet she'd be proud of me right about now.

Lucy's arms come all the way down to her sides, then she folds her hands into a neat ball in her lap. "Oh, you don't have to worry about Winnie," she says. "Winnie is getting another, *very special* honor all her own."

Winnie smiles sheepishly. "I get to be Lucy's personal serf," she gushes. "That's serf-with-an-e, not like surfing in the ocean. It's a real thing. I looked it up on Wikipedia."

Lucy St. Claire has sure got some nerve, that's all I can say. She'll have the whole stinking school waiting on her before this ball even kicks off! I can't believe I've gotten mixed up in all of this. Stella would bust a serious gut if she was here to see this going down.

"Wow, Winnie, that's…great," I stammer. "You know, if that's what you want."

"Who wouldn't want it?" she asks, throwing her arms around Lucy. "It's the greatest honor of my *whole entire life.*"

"So," Lucy says, pushing Winnie off her. "Does that mean you're in, Maggie?"

Elizabeth and Alicia are looking at me pleadingly. What choice do I have?

"Do all the days of the week end in y?" I say.

"What does *that* have to do with anything?" Lucy barks, confused. Honestly, I don't think she's the sharpest crayon in the box.

"I meant, *yes*," I say, not even believing it myself. "I'd be honored to be your…handmaiden."

Elizabeth and Alicia look like they're going to cry again—this time from relief. Lucy busts out her famously evil smirk.

"Excellent," Lucy sighs. "Now I'll take a corn dog and French fries. Oh, but you'll have to cut the corn part off, because that stuff's just nasty. Lots of ketchup too! And one of those giant chocolate chip cookies. Just tell them to put it on my account. What are you waiting for? Chop-chop! Lunch is almost over and I'm *starving*." She looks at the other girls like *can you believe she's still sitting here* and shakes her head before turning back to me. "Remember, Maggie, I can let you go at any time. Don't forget that."

I can actually hear my mom's voice inside my head. *Don't stoop to her level, Maggie. Be the bigger person.* I smile sweetly at Lucy.

"It would be my great pleasure, Your Apprenticeship," I tell her, gathering my things. "Would you like anything to drink?"

"A Coke," she says. "But not the kind with ice from the cafeteria. I like it in a can from the vending machine. I don't have any change, so you'll have to get it this time. And don't forget the straw."

Please, I add for her in my head, since it's clear she's never going to add it herself.

"Coming right up!" I chirp, winking at Elizabeth, who still looks too terrified to even think about opening her mouth.

It's not forever, I tell myself as I scrounge all of the change from the bottom of my locker. *Even though it's probably going to feel like it.*

Chapter 6

When I Get Some Not So Magical Advice from Frank-the-Genie

The corn dog was just the beginning. (And by the way, after I stripped off that greasy cornbread coating, Lucy didn't even eat the thing because guess what? A hot dog on the inside of a corn dog is not a pretty sight—it's all wrinkly and gray and looks about a hundred years old. Lucy took one look at it and flicked it by the stick in the *direction of* the trash can. When she missed, Winnie rushed over to scoop it up and sling it in the can—all with a big goofy smile across her face, of course. I guess some people are made for this sort of stuff.)

Every day this week, Lucy has come to school with a new list of tasks for us, her "lucky" handmaidens. In between carrying her books and standing in the lunch line for her, Elizabeth redecorated Lucy's locker with pink sparkly wrapping paper lining and a mini diamond tiara that she hung on a piece of fishing line like a disco ball. Alicia rode her bike to every craft store in town to find rainbow popsicle sticks for the "eat more veggies" extra-credit diorama Lucy's making for health class, and I got the honor of polishing her tennis shoes. Her tennis shoes! (I did do an excellent job, I have to admit. The secret is an old towel and toothpaste. It really gets that white to sparkle!) I guess I shouldn't complain. Lucy made poor Winnie scrub her retainer with a baby toothbrush. *Blech.*

Riding my bike home from school, all I can think about is how messed up this fake Pinkerton Princess stuff is. It's hard to believe that only a few short weeks ago, I spent a whole day as Becca Starr, the biggest rock star on the planet, and today I spent my lunch hour decorating paper bag book covers for the meanest girl in the school. It really boggles the brain.

I pull into my driveway, sling my bike behind the bushes at the front door, and let myself in with the hide-a-key. It's still a little creepy coming home to an empty house since my mom started working again. Stella usually comes over right after school to hang out with me, but she's got tae kwon do this afternoon. She thinks they're going to teach her to hover six feet off the ground. I keep telling her that's not going to happen, but she's convinced that once she reaches a certain level of *enlightenment* or something, she'll just float right up into the air when she makes the perfect kick. Well, I have to admit, stranger things *have* happened.

I shut my bedroom door, sling my backpack against it, and sit down at my vanity.

"Well?" I ask. "Aren't you going to say something, Frank?" I rest my chin in my hands and wait.

I did mention that a not-so-run-of-the-mill genie came along with the Mostly Magical Boots my Auntie Fi gave me for my birthday, didn't I? His name is Frank and he's the cowboy kind of genie—wears blue jeans instead of genie pants and a big ten-gallon cowboy hat (that's what he calls it) instead of a turban. He doesn't wear an earring that I've seen, but every once in a while, he gives out some pretty decent advice, which is something I could use right about now. Oh, and the other thing about Frank? He only shows up in a mirror. I know. It's totally kooky, but I didn't make up the way this stuff works, so I just go with it.

"I know you're dying to tell me what an idiot I am, agreeing to be the lowest life-form in the royal food chain," I say, figuring that ought to pry him away from whatever he's busy doing.

"Hey there, Maggie," Frank says with a grin as he comes into focus in the top right side of my vanity mirror. "Or are you just going by plain old Handmaiden these days?"

"Very funny," I huff.

"You'd think that girl would have come up with a better name—something to make the job sound more attractive—maybe something like 'darling duchesses' or 'happy helpers,'" Frank says, cracking himself up. "But no, she didn't even go to the trouble of putting lipstick on a pig. She just called you gals straight-up *handmaidens*. She might as well have called you her minions!"

"I *tried* not to agree to it—you know I did," I explained. "But I would've thrown my new friends under the bus. And Lucy would have torched them, for sure!"

"Uh-huh," Frank says, as a cloud of dust follows a

couple of horses pulling an old-timey-looking stage-coach right behind him.

"What the heck?" I say, leaning in to get a better look. "Where in the world are you, Frank?"

"Oh, I'm just spending a little time here in the Old Wild West, Malone," Frank says, spitting something dark and slimy out of the corner of his mouth.

"I really wish I could unsee that, Frank," I say, turning my head and gagging a little.

"It's every man for himself out here, handminion. Sink or swim. Get up or shut up," he explains as a pair of wooden doors swing behind him. "You've got to stick up for yourself in these parts or you might as well lie down and let the buzzards pick you apart."

"Um, yeah well, *that's* disgusting," I say. "It sounds really rough out there and all, Frank. But listen. I know you're probably short on time and not to be *all about me*, but can we talk about me for a sec?"

"We *are* talking about you," Frank laughs.

"What does your dirty Wild West adventure have to do with *me*, Frank?"

"Oh, I don't know, handmaiden. Are you standing up or are you lying down?" Frank asks.

"Huh?" I ask. "I'm not doing either one, Frank. I'm sitting here at my vanity talking to you!"

"Look, kid, I'm about to be late for a card game with Coyote Cain, and if I am, I'll have to start the game in my skivvies. I think you'd agree that nobody needs to see that..."

"Wait! Frank!" I yell, but it's no use.

"STAND UP, Malone!" he says, and I see him shaking his head as he goes blurry, like a watery pool. Then he's gone.

I do what he says. I stand up. But what do I do *now*? Frank just loves to pull the mysterious genie card. I think it's like his favorite thing to do. You know, toss out some crazy comments that make no sense and then leave me alone to try and piece them all together. Not to go on a Frank rant, but I always thought that genies were supposed to be at your *beck and call*. Frank is definitely not. I don't know about the beck part, but he hardly ever sticks around when I call.

Well, I knew he'd give me a hard time for going along with the crowd to keep the peace. He's always telling me to "*Stay Maggie. Be yourself*." It's true, being a handmaiden is not exactly what I'd call *being myself*. But what else was I supposed to do? And now I'm Lucy St. Claire's handmaiden for the foreseeable future.

Or. Or I could skedaddle right out of here. Leave this fake princess business behind and find out what it's like to be a *real* princess. *The* Princess Mimi to be exact, who I'm completely sure *never* has to put up with a royal pain like Lucy St. Claire pushing her around.

Chapter 7

When I Wake Up in Wincastle

Me, Maggie Malone, a *real* princess. It's going to be so great! I'll ride horses around the palace all day and have lunch with the queen and save something really important and maybe be in a parade. I've always wanted to do that princess hand-wave. Although I hope I have a bodyguard, because parades can get pretty crazy, and I know that people are always trying to kidnap famous princesses. I bet they've thought about that over in Wincastle, though.

Then I remember: the royal wedding! If I'm going to spend a day as *the* Princess Wilhelmina of Wincastle, I don't want to pick some random day when she might be stuck in her room reciting sonnets or learning French from a boring royal tutor. No way, José—I'm going to be a bridesmaid at *the royal wedding of the century*! I've only been in a wedding one time before, as a flower girl when my Grandpa Flannery got married for the tenth or eleventh time. Talk about a step up.

I turn on my computer and pull up the Celebrity Times website again, then click on the link for the royal wedding time line. As I'm scrolling through the events, I have a thought: I know that time freezes when I'm in someone else's shoes, but what about the time-difference thing? Isn't it, like, yesterday or tomorrow or something in England right now? I look it up and find out that Wincastle is exactly eight hours ahead of us. After a whole lot of adding and subtracting, I realize that if I'm going to be a bridesmaid in Princess Clementine's wedding I need to get into the MMBs pretty much RIGHT NOW!

I run over to my closet and flip on the light, then reach up to the tippy-top shelf and pull down the MMBs. *Maggie Malone, your heinie is about to be royal for real*, I tell myself, taking a deep breath before sliding one foot into a boot and then the other.

"I wish," I whisper, half nervous and half excited, "I was Princess Mimi."

* * *

What's that smell? Roses?! I *love* roses. They remind me of Granny Malone and her huge rose garden in Ireland. I open my eyes and see sweet little bouquets on each side of my bed. The bed itself has a roof and silk curtains all around it. I pull one of the curtains to the side and peek out. The ceiling is about six miles away and the entire thing—which is bigger than a football field—is covered in fancy carvings and painted *gold*.

For the love of Monopoly money, it's happening again! I'm really her. Princess Wilhelmina of Wincastle. Just like that! I whip my legs around to get out of bed and tumble down at least ten feet, landing on my hands and knees like a cat. *Really? Is this how every new day in these shoes is going to start? Besides, who needs a bed ten feet off the ground?* As I pull myself up, I see a short set of stairs Princess Mimi must use to climb in and out of this thing. That would have been good information to have a minute ago.

I walk over three miles of the cushiest carpet you ever felt to a set of huge floor-to-ceiling windows and peel back a tiny corner of a curtain that must weigh six hundred pounds. Right outside the glass and about four hundred feet down looks like a golf course—I guess that's Wincastle Palace's front lawn—and beyond that are a bunch of beautiful old buildings that belong in a fairy tale. The streets are lined with lots of tiny black cars and a few bright red double-decker buses.

I'm watching those buses creep along when the gigantic doors to my room burst open. Three ladies wearing white gloves and matching black dresses with white aprons come in.

"Good morning, Princess Wilhelmina," says the first with a quick curtsy, looking down and setting a silver tray with a lid on it beside my bed.

"Good morning, Princess Wilhelmina," says the second, also looking away as she opens all the curtains in my room. She does it quickly too, so she must be really strong.

"Oh, hey," I say, trying to remember how you say hello in British. Oh, yeah—I got it. "Cheerio, you guys!" And do you want to know the coolest thing? I have a real British accent! I don't sound a thing like Stella did the time she played Eliza Doolittle in

My Fair Lady. Or Mr. Mooney at the assembly. This is the real deal.

"Your breakfast is served, Princess," the tray lady says with a curtsy, lifting the silver lid.

A real, royal breakfast in bed? Not a bad way to start my day as a princess! I'll bet it's fit for a king! And I am capital-s STARVING. I scamper up the steps onto that giant bed and smooth the covers over my lap. *Please let it be chocolate chip pancakes and bacon,* I say silently.

I reach over and pull the tray into my lap. It's not chocolate chip pancakes *or* bacon, that's for sure. The plate is ice cold and has a handful of button mush-rooms, a shriveled-up slice of tomato that looks like somebody tried to cook it, a few baked beans, and a black blob of something that could possibly have come straight from a can of cat food.

Great. My breakfast looks like skunk meat and smells even worse. I hope this isn't a sign of things to come.

Chapter 8

When I Almost Have to Eat Blood Pudding

As I'm trying to figure out how I'm going to quietly dispose of my cat food breakfast, there's a quick knock at the door. In comes another woman, an older one, wearing a stiff skirt and buttoned-up jacket.

"Good morning, Amelia," the black-dress trio says all together.

"Good morning, Princess Mimi," she says to me first, before turning to the crew. "Ladies." They curtsy again. She notices my full tray of what I think is supposed to be food.

"If you're not hungry this morning, I shall have this taken away," this Amelia person says, looking at me oddly.

"Oh, no, sorry," I say. "I mean, I beg your pardon. I'd love a bite to eat, actually, it's just…" Man I do dig this accent of mine. I sort of want to keep talking, but I'm not sure what to say.

"The Royal Chef prepared your blood pudding just the way you like it," Amelia says, "but should you rather have something else, I can see to that right away."

Blood pudding? I think I just threw up in my mouth.

"Um, well, actually," I say, desperate to know what a princess would do in this situation. Besides eat something called blood pudding—whatever that is— because *that* is not going to happen. "Is there any… cereal or maybe a slice of toast in the palace?"

"I'll have some brought up, of course. But if it pleases the princess, perhaps you could eat it after your fitting," Amelia says. "Mr. Roberto D'Angelo is here and ready for you."

The Roberto D'Angelo, as in the legendary Italian fashion designer? He makes all the dresses that the famous actresses wear to the Big Screen Awards and he's on that show *Escape from Style Siberia*, where they rescue people from all sorts of fashion disasters.

He's kind of mean on that show, but to get to wear a dress designed by him? To the royal wedding of the century—and to be photographed and on TV in a trillion countries? What could be better than this?

"Jolly great!" I say. Last summer Stella and I found this hilarious British comedian on MeTube and watched about eleven thousand of his performances. It's coming in jolly handy already (jolly is British for *very*), and with my awesome accent and all, I'm sure I can pull this off.

Amelia nods and opens the door. When she does, Roberto D'Angelo steps into the room, wearing a long cape, dark glasses, and one of those hats that French painters wear—a beret, I think. He's followed by at least five assistants who are swarming around him like drones serving the queen bee. One assistant takes his sunglasses and swiftly replaces them with magnifying ones, while another wheels in the dress (the dress!) on a shiny brass trolley thing.

Mr. D'Angelo comes right over to me and kisses me on both cheeks. "Princess Mimi, you are a vision this morning, my dear," he gushes. "Your skin is going to be magnificent against the coral silk we've chosen for your gown, and your eyes will reflect like tropical lagoons…" he goes on and on, but I'm not listening because I keep thinking he might be the nicest guy ever—he's not behaving at all like he does on that show.

Mr. D'Angelo waves a hand and an assistant slips the dress out of its dust cover and brings it over to me. I am not exaggerating when I tell you it is the most beautiful dress I've ever seen in real life. It's made out of silk in this pale shade of peachy-pink that, if I do say so myself, will go perfectly with my strawberry-blond ringlets. It's long and fitted all the way down, with sleek cap sleeves and a square neck trimmed with the tiniest gold-ish tinted pearls.

I reach out to touch the pearls and Mr. D'Angelo says with a smile, "Sourced in Southeast Asia, just for you, Princess."

"It's just so gorgeous!" I say, throwing my arms around his shoulders, which makes all five of his assistants gasp. *What? Can't a girl show some appreciation for a job well done? Oh well, better reel it in, Malone.*

I take a step back and try to be royal. "I simply cannot wait to wear this lovely dress today, Mr. D'Angelo." Then I give him a big, deep curtsy. "Thank you so much."

"Don't be silly, Princess. You know this gown is for the London premiere of the new James Bond film next month," Amelia says with a confused chuckle, apologizing as she ushers Roberto D'Angelo and his posse out the door and shuts it behind her back.

Amelia strides over to a bag one of the glove ladies has brought in, holds the hanger in the crook of her finger, and unzips it.

Say WHAT?

Surely that thing couldn't be meant for me, Princess Wilhelmina of Wincastle!

Could it?

Chapter 9

When I See the World's Most Disappointing Dress

It's a big fat baby dress. Sort of off-white with gigantic, puffy sleeves and completely plain except for about seven hundred buttons going up the back. Oh, and a sash that I'm 100 percent sure will be tied in a huge bow above my behind. *How embarrassing.* I'm going to look like my baby cousin Caitlin at her preschool graduation. What a letdown after the totally delicious dress I just saw and will never get to wear.

Maybe the shoes will be better. They're in a beautiful silver satin box and I'm hoping they're some elegant pumps with a just-right heel that I'd never be able to wear back home. But no. I open the lid to find a pair of boring baby flats with a strap across the top. *Well, so much for making the Style File page of* Tween Scene. *I wonder if they'd ever put a princess on the Worst Dressed List.*

"It's brilliant, Amelia, really," I say, trying to sound upbeat. *It's just a dress,* I tell myself. *I'm not going to let it ruin my day.*

"I'm glad you approve, Princess," she says. "Let's just hope we can do something with that hair. Did your maids forget to braid it last night? It looks as if something could be nesting in there!"

"Umm…well," I say, running to my vanity to take a look. I have to say, she's right. Maybe switching time zones cranked up the frizz factor on my curls. I try not to panic. I'm sure the palace has someone who can fix this mess. *Okay, Malone. This is no time to get your knickers in a twist. You're a princess. Do something ROYAL!*

"I was thinking we could straighten my hair today," I say with all of the confidence I can muster. It didn't work when I was Becca Starr—turned out Becca's fans really dug these curls. I hope I'll get luckier this time around.

"You'll be wearing your hair *up* today, of course,"

Amelia says. "Are you feeling all right this morning, Princess? Forgive me, but you seem a bit…off."

Haven't even had breakfast and I'm already rocking the palace. Yikes.

"Oh, no, I'm jolly good, ma'am," I say, trying to get in the swing of things.

"I'm happy to hear that. Now let's go over your schedule. Let's see, you're set to leave the palace at precisely 9:23, and we must not be late," Amelia tells me. "That gives us exactly two hours and eleven minutes. Just a quick ride with Darling today, Princess. We've got to get you packed for your trip to the island estate tomorrow. And then we must bathe you, of course. Not a lot of time, I'm afraid."

"No problemo!" I say, since I figure princesses are probably fluent in a bunch of languages. I get to ride Darling? Princess Mimi is all into horses and Darling is her beautiful black Arabian she's always posing with in pictures. Somebody pinch me! *Wait, did she just say bathe me? As in, get lathered up like a baby? I don't think so!* Not to sound ungrateful or anything, but I think I'm perfectly capable of applying soap to my own body. I wonder if I'm allowed to do that.

"Amelia?" I say. "After we pack and take care of Darling, I was thinking I might like to *shower* this morning. By myself."

Her rosy cheeks turn as white as the inside of a York Peppermint Pattie. A hundred years later, she answers.

"As you wish," she says, backing toward my door. "I'll lay out your riding clothes now, and when we get back from the stables, I'll run your water for you."

Princesses don't even have to run their own shower water? It seems crazy to me, but seeing as I have a chore list a mile long waiting for me at home, I'm going to enjoy the royal treatment while I can.

Chapter 10

When I Have My Very Own
Black Beauty Moment

After I chow down on some delicious buttered toast, I slide into a pair of perfectly fitted riding pants with a matching jacket and pull on the most gorgeous leather boots. Feeling like a real equestrian, I follow Amelia to the fanciest golf cart I've ever seen. She starts it for me and points up toward a building in the far distance.

"I'll come for you at the stables in forty-five minutes," she says.

"Cheerio!" I tell her. I hop into this golf cart that looks like a mini Mercedes and wheel across the lawn toward the stables. The only other time I've even been on a golf cart was the time Stella and I visited her grandpa at his retirement community. Stella promised me it was totally okay for us to take his golf cart four-wheeling in the swamp behind the golf course. The security guard who found us slinging mud from the tires onto the NO CARTS BEYOND THIS POINT sign was not happy with us.

This is totally different. I'm rolling across the lawn and nobody, *I mean nobody*, is going to tell me I'm doing anything wrong because, well, I'm a princess, right? I decide to do a figure eight. I cut it a little close on one turn and almost tip the thing over, but I straighten up. I find a button that makes all the lights flash—fun! I'm trying to think of what else I ought to try while I've got this sweet little ride, but then I see her: Darling, the blackest, shiniest horse on the planet with the biggest, most sparkly brown eyes I've ever seen. When she sees me, she stomps her feet and lets out a loud horsey "Neighhhhh!"

I cannot wait to ride that horse. I'm a pretty good horse rider too. They have these ponies at our state fair every year, and I've been riding them around that circle since I was five. I walk toward Darling's stable, saying hello and cheerio to the stable people along the way. I'm settling in to the princess life quite easily, if I do say so myself.

"Brush, Princess?" a guy asks and hands me this paddle-looking thing with bristles on it.

"No thank you, kind sir," I say with a big smile. "I have someone doing my hair later this morning, I believe."

He looks confused, but then again he's a guy. He's probably never had anybody do his hair for him in his whole life.

I get to Darling's stable and I have to say, her teeth are GINORMOUS, which freaks me out since she could bite my nose off clean if she wanted to. But she'd never do that. She loves me—er, Mimi. I reach up and stroke her between the ears and she nuzzles me with her big, soft nose.

Another stable guy offers me a carrot. "Um, no thank you," I say politely. "I've just eaten breakfast." They've got some strange customs here in Wincastle— must be a princess offering thing. Who knows?

I use the stepladder and climb onto Darling's saddle. It creaks when I do and I get a whiff of leather mixed with the mounds of fresh hay on the ground. I smile at one of the stable guys waiting there and he walks Darling out to the lawn. He nods at me, and he seems like a nice enough guy so I nod back. When I do, he slaps Darling square on the rear end and we're off! Thanks for the heads-up, buddy!

At first I'm kind of terrified, because those ponies at the fair maxed out at about a half mile an hour and we're probably clocking close to twenty, but Darling gallops forward, moving in such a graceful rhythm, it feels like I've done this every morning of my life. We go up a little hill, come down, and cross a little footbridge. There's what looks like a piece of a gate sitting in the middle of a field, and I start to feel panicky when I realize that Darling is heading straight for it. I guess I'm not very good at steering—those ponies at the fair knew that circle by heart. She has to see it, right? As it gets closer and closer, I close my eyes and hold on tight, bracing for a crash, but Darling sails over that fence like the cow jumping over the moon, and my stomach flies up into my chest like the time I rode The Gasp at Rocky's Amusement Park. Forget the wedding; I think I'll spend the day with Darling, here. Unfortunately, I hear a loud horn and Darling starts booking it back to the stable. When I get there, Amelia is waiting.

"Lovely ride today, Princess," she tells me. "Now, you've thirteen minutes to pack for the island, and then it's into the shower you go."

Thirteen minutes, huh? They don't mess around over here.

"Let's do this!" I tell her. "I mean, of course. After you, Amelia."

Chapter 11

When I Meet the Devil Herself

Amelia has already laid out stacks of swimsuits and cover-ups and dresses for me to choose from in my room. I pick my favorites—although it's all a little formal for my tastes—hoping Mimi likes what I choose for her. Oh, whatever. The girl is going to be lounging on a beautiful, totally private tropical island. Who would she be trying to impress anyway?

"Now, if you please, your shower awaits," Amelia announces. "It's a perfect forty degrees."

Forty degrees? Then I remember they use that crazy Celsius system over here. Amelia hands me a velvet robe and leads me to the shower. It's all made out of marble and bigger than the group shower in the gym at Pinkerton. I could live in here, but I don't want to waste my day as a princess scrubbing my armpits, so I do my business as quickly as I can.

I open the bathroom door in a swirl of steam and bump face-first into Amelia, who is standing there with the black-dress triplets close behind her.

"I trust you had a nice shower," Amelia says, fanning at the steam. "Princess Penelope is dressed and ready, so we must hurry."

Princess Penelope is another of Mimi's cousins. She's not all over every magazine like Mimi and her cousin Clementine, so I don't know much about her. What I *do* know is it'll be great to have a friend my age to hang out with today.

Amelia hands me one of those slips like Granny Malone wears. The ladies turn their backs as I drop my towel and pull on the slip before stepping into the big fat baby dress.

I start in on those buttons, which is sort of hard to do because they're behind me and all, so I'm all twisted up like a pretzel.

"Princess Mimi, *please*," Amelia says, pushing my hands away. "Buttoning buttons is *not* the work of a princess."

Sweet Fanny Adams, what can princesses do for themselves? I hope I'm allowed to wipe my own royal heinie!

Seven hundred buttons later, Amelia guides me toward the vanity chair and begins brushing my hair out with a fancy silver brush. It's not looking half bad so I'm hoping she'll just let it be, but she takes the whole mess of it into one hand, twists it into the tightest knot possible, and begins pinning it to the nape of my neck. When she's done, I look like an alien.

"Take. Me. To. Your. Leader," I croak in my best alien-robot voice.

"I beg your *pardon*?" Amelia asks, looking a little Martian herself with her eyes bugging out like that.

"Oh, it was a…I was just…" I say. "Never mind."

Amelia shakes her head, confused. She dusts my cheeks with powder and sweeps some clear lip gloss on my lips—big whoop de do—and then whisks me down the hall. She knocks sharply on a door, and out comes Princess Penelope. She's wearing a tight little smile and the exact same alien hairdo and baby dress as me.

"Good Morning, Mimi," she purrs. "You look ever so lovely today."

"Oh, you know, thanks…" I stammer, looking down. *Who's she kidding? We both look ridiculous.* But I figure I should play along. "And so do you, er, Penny." If she calls me Mimi, I should probably call her Penny, right?

"Now, Mimi," Amelia steps in. "You know Princess Penelope prefers to be called by her given name."

"Perhaps Princess Mimi has forgotten how our barely royal third cousins Alfred and Arthur taunted me with those horrible nicknames in the country last summer," Princess Penelope says, narrowing her eyes at me. "It was so long ago. I'm sure she's forgotten."

Gulp.

"Umm, yes," I say. "I'm very sorry. I completely forgot about that. Nasty little trolls, they are!" Penelope nods, looking at least a little satisfied with me slamming our obviously annoying cousins.

"Okay, ladies," Amelia urges. "We mustn't dally. The driver is waiting." I realize that I have no idea how long we'll be in that car, and I already need to go the bathroom. Plus I wouldn't mind having a quick pep talk with Frank. I could use some solid genie advice right now. Somehow I doubt ducking into a Burger Barn is going to be an option.

"Amelia?" I ask. "Would you mind if I run to the potty, if I promise to be super quick?"

"Run to the…*potty*?" she asks.

Buggers! They don't call it the potty here, do they?

"The loo, of course," I say. "I'd like to visit the loo."

"Are you *sure* you're feeling all right this morning, Princess?" Amelia wants to know.

"Yes!" I insist. "Positively perfect. Besides having to use the loo, that is."

"Quickly, please," she tells me. "We're due to arrive at Winfordshire Abbey in less than twenty minutes, and we don't have a moment to spare."

"I'll proceed to the car then, Amelia," Princess Penelope says. "It is ever so important to respect the schedule of such events…" I hear Penelope explaining something as I rush off in search of the nearest bathroom, relieved to see there's no maid wearing rubber gloves following me with a role of monogrammed TP.

I find a loo—if you can call it that. Talk about a swanky potty. I am pretty sure this very room is why they sometimes call potties *thrones*. It has its own lobby filled with fancy armchairs and giant mirrors on every wall with gold carved frames as thick as a door. You could have a birthday party in this place!

"Hello?" I call out. "Anyone else in here?" My voice echoes around the place but nobody answers.

"Psst," I whisper into one of the mirrors. "Frank. Frank-the-genie! Come in, Frank!"

I practically have my face pressed right up against one of those huge mirrors when I spot Frank standing behind me. It freaks me out and I scream and whip around. It turns out he's not *actually* behind me, but in another one of the mirrors. It's like we're in a funhouse and he's everywhere I turn—and so am I. It's dizzying.

"Well good day there, Princess!" Frank bellows. He's wearing these tall rubber boots that come almost all the way to the top of his legs, and he's standing in what looks like a river. A blinding beam of sunlight glints off the snowcapped mountains behind him. "How's the royal life treating you so far? Better than being a handmaiden?"

"Jeez, Frank, you sure know how to scare a girl," I tell him. "Where are you this time?"

"Fly-fishing in Saskatchewan!" shouts Frank,

hauling back and casting his fishing rod far out of my line of vision. That river is moving pretty fast, and Frank looks like he could get swept away at any minute. "It's an annual thing I do with my genie buddies. We need to relax and rejuvenate too, you know, have a little downtime. You probably think being a genie is all magic mirrors and flying carpets, but honestly, it's *exhausting*." Frank is a little red in the face from tugging on his line, but still he doesn't look all that exhausted to me.

"Well, that's great, Frank," I say. "I'm fine, I guess. A little nervous about today. And that Penelope seems like she might be trouble."

"Oh, you can handle Penelope," Frank says with another laugh.

"Thanks for the vote of confidence," I say. "Any specific pointers?"

"Just be yourself, Malone," Frank says. "That's the secret to working the MMBs. If you get in a bind, don't ask yourself *what would Princess Mimi do*, ask yourself *what would Maggie Malone do*? If you do that, I promise you'll be just fine."

I don't know about that. I'm pretty sure princesses

are supposed to be polished and sophisticated, and I wouldn't say I'm *famous* for putting my foot in my mouth or anything, but let's just say I'm familiar with the move.

Before I can think of anything else to ask Frank, his reel starts making this crazy buzzing sound. The line gets really taut, and then it's dragging him away.

"Gotta run, Malone," he shouts, disappearing into the distance. "This sucker is *huge*. I think I might have a narwhal on the hook here!"

And then he's gone. I take care of my business, being extra careful to hike that gigantic bow up nice and high so it doesn't dip into the toilet. Then I wash my hands, take a deep breath, square my shoulders, and look myself right in the eyes. *You chose this, Malone. Now let's go do it!*

As I approach the waiting limousine, a guy holding the door open tells me that Amelia has gone ahead in another car, to explain the scheduling mishap. *Jeez! Not a lot of wiggle room in the life of a princess, huh?* I slide into the backseat next to Penelope, who is looking straight ahead with that weird smile on her face.

"This is going to be fantastic, don't you think?" I ask.

She turns toward me. Her face looks as if she's just sucked on a lemon slice.

"If by fantastic you mean that you'll be escorted down the aisle by Prince Albert's amazingly handsome son Prince Henry, while I'll be forced to lock arms with horrible Lord Harold of Southumberland, then yes, *positively fantastic*," Penelope hisses.

Whoa! What's that *all about? Is this because I called her Penny? Big, blooming deal!* I assume she's done chewing me out, but apparently she's not.

"And if by fantastic you mean that *you'll* be positioned front and center for all the international press to photograph, while *I'll* be tucked away out of sight like a complete commoner, then yes," she seethes, "this will be fantastic. Fantastic for *you*."

I'm about to respond, but she's *still* not finished. "And if you think you're going to be the center of attention at this wedding like you've been at every other affair in your entire spoiled life, you've got another thing coming, my *noble* cousin." She's practically shouting at me now, and she says *noble* like it's an insult. Her cheeks are burning with disgust.

Double gulp. She's not just a little bit peeved with me—I

mean Mimi. She hates her stinking guts. Like, wants to rip her heart out and stomp it into the floor mats of this really fancy car. I am burnt toast. Where is the button I press to go back to being plain old Maggie Malone?

Frank-the-genie made it clear that once I pick a pair of shoes to step into, they're mine for the rest of the day, no take backs. But he didn't mention anything about becoming somebody else only find out that *another* somebody wants *that* somebody D.E.A.D.

Chapter 12

When I Am Nearly Killed by a Scone

My mouth is hanging open and I'm wondering what I could possibly say to make Princess Penelope hate me a little less when I hear a man's voice coming from the front of the limo.

"Everything all right back there, Your Highnesses?" he asks, lowering the glass between us just a few inches.

Penelope glares at me.

"Oh! Umm… we're grand, thanks," I say. "Just joking around, you know. Giving each other the old punch in the gut."

"Very well," he says, raising the glass again.

"Oh, so that's how it's going to be now?" Penelope says. I don't have time to ask her what she means by that, because right then, we pull up in front of Winfordshire Abbey.

I have never seen a building like this in my life! It's the size of thirty churches all smushed together, with towers and arches and ten thousand spiky things sticking up out of the top. It looks like a fort or a fortress, and not one tiny bit like the Buffalo Lodge where Grandpa Flannery's gotten hitched at least half a dozen times.

A man in a fancy red suit and hat opens the limo door, and I get out and join the other bridesmaids. There are six of them and they are all wearing the same buttoned-up baby dress as me and Penelope. Crowds of people are lined up behind metal gates, screaming at me like I'm a famous rock star or something. I notice that Penelope hasn't gotten out of the limo. *That's weird. Maybe she's really nervous or got snatched up by aliens or something.* I won't tell you which one I'm hoping for.

I grin like a crazy person and lift my right arm to give the famous princess wave. I keep smiling and start tilting my head and turning my hand left to right. I'm really getting into it when out of nowhere, Amelia rushes over, puts a giant silk cape over my shoulders, and practically pushes me into the abbey.

What gives? That was really fun! I was having my first real Princess Mimi moment!

"Unfortunately, it seems you've sat in something vile and it has attached itself to your backside," Amelia says, looking horrified.

"What? How could that have—" I crane my neck around to have a look. I feel dizzy when I see it: a blob of…it looks like *peanut butter*…the size of Texas smeared across my butt. And it just so happens I am *deathly* allergic to peanut butter.

"Oh my goodness, Amelia, I can't…" I gasp, grabbing her arm to keep myself from falling. "I can't… breathe. And why is the room spinning like that? Who turned off the lights? I'm going to die! I'm going to *die*!!!"

"Princess Wilhelmina, get hold of yourself," she says sternly, gripping my shoulders. "As disastrous as this is, I am fairly certain that a bit of molasses is not going to *kill* you."

"Molasses?" I ask. "What is? But how? I didn't—"

Just then Princess Penelope bursts into the abbey.

"Oh, Mimi, I heard what happened," she says. "How terribly awful of me to leave my scone on the limousine seat like that. Is there anything I can do? I am so, *so* very sorry." The funny thing is, she doesn't look—or sound—one tiny bit sorry.

"What's done is done," Amelia says. "It's a good thing the Crown Cape lives here at Winfordshire Abbey."

"She gets to wear the *Crown Cape*?" Penelope spits, her face turning practically purple. "All day long? Surely you don't mean in the *actual wedding*?"

"Have you another idea, Penelope?" Amelia asks, pointing at my backside.

"But the Crown Cape belongs to Her Majesty the Queen!" Penelope cries. "If Mimi wears it, everyone will think she's the queen's favorite."

"So be it," Amelia says, turning from Penelope and fastening the cape's jeweled clasp at my neck.

Penelope squares her shoulders and looks me dead in the eye. *You'll be sorry*, she mouths before marching off to join the rest of the bridal party.

Is this royally happening?

"Try not to sit in anything else sticky," Amelia scolds as she steers me to the altar where the wedding party is lining up for pictures. "There's no backup Crown Cape, you know."

Half of England is standing in near-perfect rows across the altar of Winfordshire Abbey. Amelia leads me to one side and I fall into line, toward the back.

"Lovely, brilliant," says the photographer. "But Princess Wilhelmina? Kindly move to the front row, center. Yes, right there in Princess Clementine's spot. We mustn't let that Crown Cape get lost in these photographs. That's it. Now a bit to the left. Ah, jolly good! A few close-ups of you now for the media, Princess Wilhelmina."

Something tells me Princess Penelope is going to make me pay for this, I think, taking a deep breath and plastering a smile across my face.

Chapter 13

When I Sort of Save the Day

After ten kajillion pictures—and as many evil glares from Penelope—it's finally time for the actual Royal Wedding. The moment I've been waiting for! Sure, I'm a little nervous—but really, how badly could I mess this up?

Even though it's the size of a mall, Winfordshire Abbey is packed like a can of sardines with women in crazy hats with feathers and wings and gigantic bows and men who look like they just stepped out of *The Nutcracker*. This Wincastle place sure has a weird sense of style.

All of us big-fat-baby-dresses are in the back, being paired up with our escorts. An orchestra starts playing this creepy, sleepy music as Amelia shuffles us into position. She fluffs the Crown Cape so that it drapes perfectly around my shoulders, with the bottom pooling softly at my feet.

Suddenly the organ plays three sharp notes, and every person in the abbey stands. You could hear a pin drop in this place. A side door opens and in walks Clementine's uncle, Prince Alexander, and on his arm is Her Royal Majesty Queen Millicent III. She's, like, the mother of all royalty! My mom has a plate with her face on it and I'm right here in the same room with her. I swear, sometimes this whole MMB thing is hard even for *me* to believe.

Once Her Royal Majesty is seated, it's showtime. Prince Henry and I are second in line, just behind the flower girl and the ring bearer. Princess Penelope and Lord Harold are right behind us.

The flower girl, Princess Sophie, is the cutest little thing I have ever seen. She's got these rosy cheeks and this golden blond hair that she gets to wear down (lucky!). Of course she's wearing the big fat baby dress too—but she looks like an angel in hers, especially with that pretty wreath of flowers on top of her head. It looks like a halo. Her brother, Prince Valdemar, has the same golden hair and a dusting of freckles across his little button of a nose.

It's hard to believe these two kids might be running a whole country someday. They're just too cute for words.

The organ strikes up a new song, and the lady in charge of the little kids gives them a gentle nudge. Prince Valdemar has his arm linked in Princess Sophie's. They look like a miniature bride and groom. I just want to pinch their adorable little cheeks.

"No, Henrietta!" Princess Sophie says suddenly.

"What do you mean *no*?" Henrietta, Princess Sophie's governess, asks.

"I'm not going!" Princess Sophie says, even louder this time.

"You're *not going*?" Henrietta whispers back, confused.

"I am not going down that aisle and you can't make me," Princess Sophie says. With her British accent, she sounds exactly like that bratty I-want-an-Oompa-Loompa-*now* girl from *Willy Wonka & the Chocolate Factory*.

"Of course you are, dear," says Henrietta, giving her another push.

"Am not, am not, am not!" Princess Sophie screams. She's waving her arms and jumping up and down, and people in the abbey begin to turn around. Poor Prince Valdemar is looking down at his shiny shoes and trying not to cry.

"Princess Sophie, I have had *enough of this behavior*," Henrietta whispers angrily, grabbing her tiny arm. "You are expected to act like a lady at all times, and you will obey my orders, do you hear me?"

"I am not going and you cannot make me, Henrietta hog face!" Princess Sophie yells this last bit at full volume, and the entire abbey full of guests gasps at the same time. Now every head is twisted around to watch the show. Henrietta's nose does turn up a bit at the end, but I think "hog face" is a little harsh.

"Princess Sophie," I whisper, kneeling down. "What's the matter? Are you nervous about going down the aisle?" She nods her head and a tear slips down her cheek.

"I am too," I tell her with a wink. She smiles a thin, close-lipped smile. "I'll bet Princess Clementine is more nervous than both of us put together, don't you think?"

Princess Sophie nods her head and wipes the tear away with the back of her hand.

"And what do you suppose would happen if *she* refused to go down the aisle?" I ask her.

"There wouldn't be a royal wedding at all!" the little princess mumbles, looking down sadly.

"We wouldn't want to give her any ideas then, would we?" I ask.

"No, I suppose not," she agrees. "But I still can't do it."

"Of course you can," I tell her gently.

"But I haven't any teef," she says, looking up at me and opening her mouth widely. She's got a huge hole where her two front teeth should be.

"Oh, sweetie, you lost your front teeth!" I say, all excitedly. "That's fantastic! Congratulations! Have you shown Princess Clementine yet? That's very good luck on a wedding day, you know."

"It is?" she asks, looking a tiny bit hopeful.

"Oh yes," I say, scrambling to make up a good story. "Yes, when someone in the wedding party loses a tooth just before the wedding, it's a sign that the bride and groom will live a long, happy, smiling life together."

"I didn't know that!" she says with a big grin.

"How lucky is Princess Clementine?" I ask her. "And all because of you. Now don't forget to smile really big when you walk down that aisle, so everyone can see all of that good luck."

She nods at me, then slips her arm back through Prince Valdemar's. He's grinning like a fool.

"Leave the smiling to me, Valdemar," Princess Sophie tells her brother, giving his arm a nice tug.

"Well, look who just saved the day," Princess Penelope hisses into my ear. I pretend not to hear her. Right now, all I care about is getting down this aisle without tripping or fainting, like you always see on TV.

Chapter 14

When I Am Practically Strangled to Death

Princess Sophie is really working the crowd with that smile, so it takes her and Prince Valdemar about a year to get to the altar. The waiting is killing me. Let's get this show on the road, people! I only have one day as Princess Mimi, and I'd rather not spend it standing in the back of an abbey, even if it is a really famous and beautiful one.

Finally the little kids are at the altar. Amelia gives me a weak smile and a tiny nod.

"Princess?" whispers Prince Henry, offering me his arm. Not to be all gushy, but Penelope was right: Henry is way cuter than Lord Harold. In fact, he might be the cutest boy I have ever seen. Way cuter than Jake Ritchie and maybe even cuter than Justin Crowe. I link my arm with his and smile nervously. My knees are wobbling and my hands feel like two wet noodles. I can feel Penelope's hot, angry breath on my neck, but there's nothing I can do about it.

Settle down, you silly stomach butterflies. I won't let you ruin my royal moment!

With my arm linked in Prince Henry's, I take my first step forward. At least I try to, but suddenly I feel as if I'm being strangled and I start to tip backward. I squeeze Prince Henry's arm tighter, gasping for air, and try to straighten back up.

Am I fainting? It happens all the time in weddings on that show *Real Funny Videos*. Usually it's the groom who goes down, though, and normally it's during a really boring part of the wedding. I haven't even made it out of the gate!

I try to take a step again but something is seriously strangling me.

That wicked witch is trying to kill me, I realize. *She's wrapped her paws around my neck and I'm going to die right here in Winfordshire Abbey. In this hideous, horrible, big fat baby dress! With a kazillion people watching!*

She wouldn't do that, would she? I mean, she's

definitely awful, but I think murder is too evil—even for Princess Penelope.

I wave my one free arm wildly. It's as if there's a rope around my neck and someone is yanking on it as hard as they can. It's no use fighting it; the pull is too strong. I'm starting to see stars and the room is beginning to spin. I'm tipping back and I can't stop it, and everything feels like it's in slow motion.

I hope my underwear isn't showing when I land, is all I can think. I stop waving my free arm and use it to hold down the front of my big fat baby dress, just in case.

Wow, the ceiling of this abbey is amazing, I notice as I continue to tip.

Right before I hit the ground, Prince Henry figures out what's going on and sweeps me back upright. His arm locked tightly with mine, he gives the back of the Crown Cape a nice tug with his other hand. I can breathe again! I shake my head to get some blood back into it. The abbey comes back into focus and I realize I'm not going to die in a big fat baby dress. Oh, happy day.

"I beg your pardon," Princess Penelope whispers sweetly into my ear. "It seems I was accidentally standing on the Crown Cape! Silly, careless me. Carry on, please."

"You, Penelope, are rotten to the core," Prince Henry hisses over his shoulder. "You always have been and you always will be. You are a disgrace to the crown and to all of Wincastle as well. If I weren't a gentleman, I'd tell you precisely what horrible hopes I have for you."

Prince Henry turns to me, his face a sea of big green eyes with the sweetest smile I have ever seen. "Now, if you are ready, Princess Mimi, I'd be honored to walk a true princess down the aisle as she deserves."

I nod furiously, because I don't trust myself to speak at the moment and I don't know what else to do. I don't dare look back at Princess Puckerface, that's for sure. Instead, I take a deep breath and take my first actual step down the aisle. I am arm-in-arm with the handsomest prince in all of England, the Crown Cape swishes prettily behind me, and not one person in that abbey knows about the Texas-size stain across my backside. My smile must be even bigger than Princess Sophie's. *Good always beats evil*, I think in my head.

It turns out, evil doesn't give up all that easily.

Chapter 15

When I Almost Choke on a Lamb

I've heard that royal weddings last for all of ever, but this one is taking even longer. The guy running the show is some big, important archbishop who is droning on like a human noise machine. I'm worried I'm going to fall asleep—or worse, get hypnotized like Stella did the time that famous magician came to school. He had her clucking like a chicken across the gymnasium floor. I am pretty sure that would not go over well here.

Finally, after some stuff in Latin that I don't get *at all*, the archbishop declares Princess Clementine and Prince Clayton husband and wife. *Oh boy*, I think. *Here comes the kissing part.* The bride and groom lock lips, and it's actually pretty sweet.

An organ blares and scares me so badly I let out a little yelp, but nobody seems to notice. Next thing I know, Prince Dreamy Green Eyes offers me his arm (yes, please!) to usher me back up the ten-mile aisle. I'm blinded by flashbulbs as we make our way out of Winfordshire Abbey and into the horse-drawn carriages waiting outside.

The carriages are all four-seaters, and wouldn't you know it? Prince Henry and I get tucked into seats right across from Princess Penelope and Lord Harold. She's totally ignoring the poor guy.

"So, Harold, how are things down in Southumberland?" I ask. When I do, he leans forward, almost into my lap. Talk about a close-talker. We used to call that *popping somebody's bubble* in preschool and you could get sent to the middle of the rainbow carpet for that.

"Positively perfection, Princess!" he tells me, spraying my face with spit. I'm blinking and twitching, trying to dodge the spray. "It's plum season, as you know. And I've been pestering Princess Penelope here," he says, turning his sprinkler her way, "to pay us a particularly overdue visit."

Penelope wipes her face with a handkerchief and gives me the stink eye. I just smile back at her, because what else can I do?

The carriage takes us back to Wincastle Palace. I guess there's a party that all of England is invited to later tonight, but first there's a private luncheon just for the royal family. I hope they serve steak. I had the best steak I've ever eaten in my life at one of Grandpa Flannery's weddings. It was the perfect shade of pink and tasted like grilled butter and you didn't even really have to chew it because it melted right in your mouth. I'll never forget that steak.

Amelia meets us at the carriage and escorts us to the formal dining room. It's the fanciest place I have ever seen in my life. It's got the same billion-foot ceiling as Mimi's bedroom—maybe taller—and dark red velvet walls and curtains. Every few feet on one wall is a painting of some old man or lady (dead kings and queens, I'm guessing). They're those creepy kinds of paintings where the eyes follow you wherever you go. I try not to make eye contact with any of them.

There is one gigantic table in the middle of the room with maybe fifty chairs around it. Amelia steers us toward the table, where there are little name cards at each seat. Wouldn't you know it, there is Princess Penelope's place…right next to Princess Wilhelmina.

Can a pretend princess ever *get a royal break?*

To my surprise, Princess Penelope pulls my chair back from the table. She nods at it and smiles, and I feel a tiny bit of relief. Maybe she's gotten all that meanness out of her system and wants to be friends now. That sure would be nice. I mouth the words "thank you" and sit down.

"PRINCESS MIMI, what in heaven's name are you *doing*?" Amelia has my shoulders in her hands and is yanking me out of my chair.

"It has my name…Penelope pulled…I was just going to sit…" I try to explain.

"Nobody sits down before Her Majesty the Queen sits, Mimi!" Amelia says. "You know that!"

"I'm so sorry, Amelia," I tell her. "It won't happen again." So much for being best buds with Puckerface. That is so not going to happen. If I had a piece of red string, I'd tie it around my finger so I'd never, ever forget that.

We all stand around for an eternity, waiting for

the queen, who I think is Mimi's great-aunt, but I'm not picking up on a lot of warm, fuzzy feelings in this family, so it's sort of hard to tell if they're actually related. Finally the queen comes in and makes this big production out of lowering herself into her chair. Big royal deal! If I were a queen, I'd be all, "Hey guys, don't wait for me! Sit down! Take a load off!" Still, mine is the last butt to hit a seat in this room. I'm not taking any chances.

This table is *ridiculous*. Each one of us has a stack of four plates, three forks, and a half dozen drinking glasses. I'm just hoping that dinner is not at all like breakfast because I am so hungry I could eat an entire extra-large pizza all by myself.

"Crab mousse," announces a man in a tall white chef hat. As he does, fifty waiters—we each have our own waiter?!—set down a plate on top of the stack.

I said I could eat an entire pizza. Crab mousse? P-U! Thanks, but no thanks. And how am I going to get out of this? Too bad the palace doesn't have a dog running around. Willy comes in really handy at home in situations like this.

At least it's only one little scoop of the stinky stuff.

I look around and everyone is holding their spoon up and looking at the queen. She takes her sweet time putting that silver spoon in her mouth, I've got to tell you. Finally she sticks it in there and everyone else does the same thing—all at the exact same time. I figure it's best to just get it over with, so I jam mine in my mouth too.

It's actually not that bad. Kind of weird and salty and creamy but not totally disgusting. Lord Harold thinks this stuff is the cat's pajamas.

"Positively stupendous, wouldn't you say, Princess?" Lord Harold says, gobbling up his last bite of mousse. It looks like down in South-wherever-this-dude-is-from, they don't teach the kids to chew with their mouths closed. Yuck. Not only that, but I'm starting to realize that Lord Harold is what you'd call super-impressed with himself.

"So, Princess Penelope, have you heard about the new stables we've at Kensington Plantation? They are quite possibly perfection and I know how you adore horses, Princess," Lord Harold says, leaning ever closer like he doesn't have a clue that Penelope might at any moment rip his spitting, sputtering lips right off his face.

"No, Lord Harold, we have not heard about the new stables, but please, do tell," Penelope says, rolling her eyes. "I'm sure, like all of your stories, it will be quite thrilling."

"Well," Lord Harold says, smiling and making this exaggerated yawning motion and throwing both arms up into the air. Then he drops his right arm right down around Penelope's shoulder, like he's Mister Cool making his move. I guess Lord Harold has a sweet spot for super-mean girls. Penelope flings his paw off her shoulder with so much force that it almost knocks the tray out of one of the waiter's hands.

Lord Harold chuckles a little, and for a skinny second, I think he might be uncomfortable, but then he continues talking, clueless as to how she just cut him to the core.

"Well, as you know, the Hadley family spares no expense—we don't have to since my great grandfather laid all the railroads in South Africa back in the late 1800s…"

"Yes, yes, we know, Harold, and your family revolutionized the sugarcane industry and your father is the richest man—royal or otherwise—in the entire

United Kingdom," Penelope yawns. "You've been telling us this story since you were seven years old."

Harold yammers—or should I say, spatters—on and on about his prosperous family's positively blah, blah, blah new stables. This kid is unbelievable. He reminds me of Stella's ten-year-old cousin, Calvin, who brags about being smarter than 80 percent of all adults just because he went on some stupid quiz show and won a blow-up pool. Stella says she came *this close* to giving him an atomic wedgie at the family reunion last summer. Now I know how she feels.

Just then, Prince Henry leans over my way and whispers so only I can hear, "He really is quite horrid, isn't he?"

"Uh, well, I..." I stammer because I'm not sure if I should agree. "He sure seems to think he's something special."

"Yes, well, we all know where he gets that, don't we?" Henry continues, pointing in the direction of the Hadley family. And holy smokes, Lady Hadley is laughing with her head arched back, wearing the biggest, craziest hat in the whole place with about a gazillion feathers exploding out of the top of it.

It looks like Lord Hadley is wearing his wife's scarf tucked into the top of his shirt. He's also got just half of a pair of glasses on his face.

"What's the deal with those half glasses?" I ask Henry. "Didn't the rabbit in *Alice in Wonderland* wear one of those?"

Henry laughed. "Ridiculous, right?" he says, shaking his head. "And I'm sure his monocle belonged to his fabulously wealthy father—or his great-great-grandfather or something like that. They're really quite showy down in Southumberland. The Hadley family is, anyway."

I look up and the waiters are all lining up for the next course. I'm crossing my fingers there's a big, juicy steak heading for my plate.

"Lamb in mint sauce," announces the chef guy as our servers set down the next course. *Blimey!* See, I'm not exactly a vegetarian back home, but I do have one rule: I don't eat cute animals. Rabbit, deer, goose, lamb, all of them, out of the question. I tried to give up beef for a while—I actually do think cows are pretty cute—but by then I'd already had that wedding steak. Plus we have a Burger Barn right next door to school, so that didn't really work out for me.

I stare at my plate. Two long bones with big hunks of meat are crisscrossed on it, and the whole thing is swimming in green goo. The queen delicately slices off a chunk of meat and the rest of the room does the same. She pops it into her mouth and sighs happily. Everyone else follows. Except me. I just can't do it.

"Is there something wrong with your lamb, Princess Mimi?" Penelope asks with a big smirk. "If so, I'll be happy to alert the chef."

Sorry, my fleecy little friend, I think to myself, shoving a bite into my mouth. It's horribly sweet, and the mint makes it taste like those Life Savers Granny Malone always keeps in her purse. Who puts *mint* on top of meat, anyway? I chew and I chew, but my throat seems to have forgotten how to swallow. It's all I can do not to gag.

I smile sweetly at Penelope and keep right on chewing. I'm trying to figure out how I can spit this minty wad into my napkin when I hear fifty forks being placed on their plates. The queen has stopped eating—which means we have to stop too. Make that, we *get* to stop. I grab my water goblet and take a huge swig, and then another. Finally that meat goes down.

I make a promise right then and there that I will never complain about my mom's meatloaf ever again.

Dessert is cherries jubilee, and while cherries aren't exactly my favorite (I normally pluck the cherry off the top of a hot fudge sundae and give it to Mickey or Stella), after that Life Saver lamb, I'm grateful for any other taste in my mouth. Most of all, I'm glad this meal is just about over. The reception will be the fun part. Plus I'll have room to roam and I can stay far, far away from Princess Penelope.

Chapter 16

When I Get My Groove On

After the luncheon, the wedding party is led to the part of Wincastle Palace's golf-course-sized yard known as "the meadow" for what Amelia tells me will be an eight-hour reception. *Eight hours?* I'm hoping we get another meal or else I might pass out on the dance floor.

Talk about tents! It looks like the circus has come to town—all of them in the world, all at once. As we trot through the tent city to our assigned seats, there are cheers all around. Yes, princesses get applause just for showing up and being born royal.

Everyone stands as the Archduke of Wincastle introduces the bride and groom. Cousin Clementine really does look beautiful and her new husband Prince Clayton isn't bad either—except for that shock of neon red hair on his head. Yowza! I wonder if it glows in the dark. That would be all kinds of awesome at Friday night Glo-Bowl.

The bride and groom have their first dance. It's pretty magical. She's as graceful as a ballerina, and they both move like those professional dancers on TV. When they're finished, people start flooding out onto the dance floor.

Prince Henry turns to me. I have to say, it's not just those sparkly green eyes or that adorable grin or those Chiclet-white teeth that get me with this guy. Those things are nothing compared to how nice and well, *charming* he is. My mom is always saying that it's what's inside that counts, and she must be right because Prince Henry makes me go all gooey inside.

"So, what's your favorite dance of the moment, Princess?" Prince Henry asks. "Everyone knows you to be the best dancer in all of Wincastle."

"Me?" I answer. I didn't know this about Princess Mimi! "A great dancer? Aw, well, you know…"

I'm really wishing I'd taken my mom up on those fancy dance classes she wanted me to take back in fourth grade. I'd thrown a bit of a hissy fit about going after my big cousin Clare told me how the boys' sweaty hands get the girls' white gloves all slimy. Blech! Mom finally caved in and said I didn't have to go. She said I would regret it someday, though, and I do. Right about now.

"Your modesty is most endearing, Princess," Henry says, standing and pulling my chair back. "A dance of your choosing, if you please. You lead and I'll follow."

Penelope doesn't look happy at all, which gives me just the courage I need to march onto the dance floor. I'll show that cruel cousin of mine how it's done.

As Prince Henry leads me by the small of my back toward the dance floor, I start flipping through my brain trying to think of some dances I know. Wait a minute! Stella and I learned the Cowgirl Booty Scoot on MeTube last summer. I'm really good at that! There's a lot of kicking and twisting, though. I wonder if I can pull that off with this heavy cape around my neck. But when you think about it, what choice do I have?

"I don't know if you know this one, Henry, but it's pretty easy," I whisper as we reach the edge of the black-and-white marble dance floor. "I'm sure you'll catch on quickly. Just hang on a second!"

I race over to the orchestra and ask a guy who's sort of hanging out to one side if they can play something country. He looks at me like I'm crazy.

"Country and western?" I have to yell over the music so he can hear me. "You know, cowboys, horses, pickup trucks. Country!"

"Oh!" he shouts back with a smile. "I believe we can do that, Princess Mimi!"

After some whispering and flipping of sheet music, the musicians start playing a twang-y sort of song. It's not one I know, but it sounds like it'll do.

I pull Prince Henry out to the middle of the dance floor and count off in my head just like Stella and I do before we start our routine. *Five, six, seven, eight.* I start with a smooth slide to the right and a clap, then put my hands on my hips and I slide back to the left. Next I do what's called a kick-ball-change two times to the right. Then I shake my shoulders. And shake my shoulders some more. Forward and back with more claps in between. This bit's a little tricky. The key is to get really loose. So that's what I do.

People are starting to leave the dance floor—they probably feel bad since I know this dance so well—but I'm too focused on my moves to give it another thought. I do one more kick-ball-change to the left before I hit my favorite part, where you slap yourself on the booty just before you turn to the right and start the whole thing over again.

This is awesome! I'm totally loose, shaking my shoulders, leaning down and then up, when I look over to see if Prince Henry is getting into it yet. He most definitely is not. He's actually just standing there with his mouth hanging open. Obviously he's amazed by my killer moves.

I glance around the room. A few people are staring, some are whispering and pointing, and Penelope is doubled over laughing. Maybe this *isn't* the best dance to be doing at a royal wedding, now that I think about it. But it's all I know. And I always stick to what I know.

Henry hesitates a little and then comes over to me. "I'm so sorry, but I'm not at all familiar with this dance, Princess," he yells. "Would you mind showing me that turning bit again?"

I count in my head again (*five, six, seven, eight*) then

I start at the beginning, but more slowly this time. It takes him a few tries, but Henry gets the steps down and then he starts getting into it too. When he does, a bunch of the wedding party trickles over with their dates, and Henry and I teach them the steps. Pretty soon we've got at least four lines of people dancing. And then the dance floor is packed with dancers clapping and laughing and slapping their booties.

I'm having the best time in all of history when I see the queen stand up. It looks like she's walking straight toward me, but I'm crossing my fingers that she's just going to the loo or checking out the cake table or something. But she's not.

"So, Princess," says Her Royal Highness the Queen of Wincastle, coming to a full stop right in front of my face. "What do you call this dance?"

"This is the Cowgirl Booty Scoot, Your Majesty!" I answer, all out of breath.

She lifts her eyebrows and nods and then—and I know this is hard to believe but I triple pinkie promise you it happens—she starts dancing. In line. Right next to me.

"Oh my, Princess," the Queen of Wincastle says

with a laugh. "It is quite amusing!" And then she *smacks her royal booty*, right there for all of Wincastle to see.

The dance floor is a total mob scene. In fact, Penelope is practically the only wedding guest not out here slapping her backside. I see Lord Harold leave the floor to invite her to dance, but she just smacks his hand away. I can't help but find it absolutely hilarious how much Lord Harold seems to love Penelope. *Positively priceless!* I think to myself and laugh out loud, but no one can hear me over all the stomping and booty slapping.

Eventually, the orchestra slides into a slow song— probably a waltz or something like that—and the dance floor starts to clear because booty-slapping *is* pretty exhausting. I'm pooped. I plop down in a comfy, out-of-the-way chair to catch my breath. About three whole minutes pass before I look up to see Prince Henry smiling down at me with two tall glasses of ice water and the cutest sideways grin I ever saw.

Chapter 17

When I Find Out the MMBs Come with a Catch

"You look to be one thirsty princess," Henry says, handing me the ice water, which I immediately put to my forehead because this big fat baby dress is made of the kind of silk that traps in all the heat. It's like an EasyDoesIt Oven under these bajillion buttons. I can't believe my knickers aren't sliding right off.

"Would you care to get some fresh air, Mimi?" he asks. Without having to think about it at all, I float up from my chair and take his arm.

We walk just outside the tent, and I swear it feels about a hundred degrees cooler out here. It really is a beautiful night—like one of those nights you see in a movie where there's not a cloud in the sky, the stars are blinking, and a big white moon looks like a spotlight on the pond until a swan swims by and leaves little waves in his wake. Seriously? It's like I'm in a fairy tale. And *hello*, I *am* chatting with a handsome prince out here so…

"Mimi?" Henry says, leaning forward to get my attention.

"Huh?" I say.

"You look like you're a hundred miles away," he says with a smile.

"Oh, I just…I…I was just thinking it's such a pretty night," I say, shaking my head a little. *Wake up, Malone! Be royal!*

"Can I ask you a question, Mimi?" Henry says, strolling as we talk.

"Yeah, I mean, of course, Henry," I say, remembering to talk like a princess. "What is it?"

"It's just…I just…well, I wanted to say that you've seemed quite different today. More…I don't know… and please don't take this the wrong way, but more fun?" he says with a grin, tilting his head to the side as we walk. "Perhaps, more real? I don't know what I'm trying to get at. I guess I wanted to say that I've really enjoyed your company today."

"Awww, Henry," I say, hitting him hard in the arm. "That's so sweet!" I don't know why I do that—punch a guy in the arm after he says something nice to me. It's like a twitch or a nervous habit or something, sort of like the way I chew the inside of my cheek when I talk to a cute boy, which I'm trying really *really* hard not to do right now.

"Wow!" Henry says, rubbing his shoulder. "That's quite a left hook you've got there, Princess!"

"Sorry!" I say. *Really, Malone? Did you have to punch the prince?* I sure know how to mess up a fairy-tale moment.

"Shouldn't you be saving the punches for your sweet cousin?" Henry asks, laughing. "You two have been what I would *almost* call civil all day long—at least *you* have been. It's like she's not getting to you today, no matter what she does. You're a true princess, Mimi, through and through. And an incredible person on top of that. And today you proved it."

"Oh, well, I...thanks, Henry," I stammer. *I'm totally tongue-tied because first of all, a REAL-LIFE PRINCE just called me incredible. Me! And second of all, I can't believe that Mimi has a part in this crazy cousin-feud too! And here I was, turning my cheek—over and over— thinking the problem was all Penelope.* I must look as flustered as I feel, because Prince Henry reaches for my hand, and when he does, I chomp down hard on my cheek. This time I get my tongue too. I've really got to work on that.

"Are you all right, Mimi?" Prince Henry asks, adorably concerned.

"Um, yeah, I'll be right back, okay?" I say through a close-lipped smile, hoping no blood is seeping out. I grab the sides of my puffy dress and run across the lawn behind the tent where a bunch of servers are shuffling back and forth. I find a parked linen truck and twist the little side mirror around so I can stick out my tongue and survey the damage.

"ACKKKKKKKKKKKKKKK!" I scream when I see Frank's face in there. He's laughing and sticking his tongue right back out at me.

"Frank, what are you *doing* here?" I whisper, looking around to see if my little explosion attracted any attention. Fortunately, the party sounds drowned me out.

"Just checking in, Malone," Frank says with a sly grin. "Everything going okay?"

"Well, obviously Penelope and Mimi have this serious rivalry thing going on. But guess WHAT? Turns out, the meanness goes both ways. Only I've been all *give Penelope another chance, she'll come around, don't make any waves.* And she's just getting worse by the second. It's like the more I let her get away with, the more evil she becomes!"

"You hit the nail on the head with that one, Malone," Frank says, pulling a nail from the side of his mouth and hammering it into a board with three hard whacks. "Get it? Hit the nail? I crack myself up, honestly."

"What are you *doing*, Frank?" I ask. I swear I don't think I've seen that guy in the same place twice.

"Oh, just a little home repair work for my cousin, Ishmael," Frank explains. "He's not very handy with a hammer, but if you want a magic carpet ride, he's your guy. Anyway, you know what you have to do, and it'll be good practice too...*Handmaiden.*"

"Oh, yeah, *that*," I say, rolling my eyes. "Thanks for reminding me, Frank. And yeah, I'll have to deal with that when I get home, but if these girls want to fight like two cats in a bag, it's not like there's anything I can do to stop them. Besides, my day as Mimi is almost over, so she'll just have to figure this mess out herself!"

"Actually," Frank says, putting his hammer down. "That's not how it works."

"What is *that* supposed to mean?" I demand.

"Here's the thing, Malone, and I feel a little bad about not mentioning this sooner, but in order for you to keep taking the MMBs for a spin, you have to affect each life you try on in some positive way. Magic has a price."

"Wait, *what*?" I ask. "You didn't tell me that! I could lose my MMBs?!"

"Well, yeah, that's sort of the point of all of this. And you did that, no problem, when you were in Becca Starr's shoes," Frank says, looking guilty. "So you need to figure out a way to bring Mimi and Penny together, help them see eye to eye. These girls have been at each other since they were in nappies—that's British for diapers. They sure do have some funny words, don't they? Anyway, they'll probably keep going at it till they're knocking wheelchairs unless they learn to get along. And somebody's got to be the bigger person to make that happen. I believe that person is you, Maggie Malone."

"So I need to patch things up between these two princesses or it's bye-bye MMBs? In the next *hour*? How am I supposed to do *that*? I don't want to lose them—you know I don't—but that's a pretty tall order, Frank!"

"You'll figure something out," Frank says. "I don't doubt it for one second." Before I can tell him he's officially nuts, somebody cranks the linen truck's engine and I barely have time to jump out of the way before it pulls away, the tailgate flapping in the breeze.

Chapter 18

When I Stick to What I Know

I make my way back toward the tent, but I don't see Henry outside anymore. He must have gone back in—or maybe he's hiding somewhere. I wouldn't blame him. I did act a little freaky when he touched my hand. Inside the tent, the orchestra has switched back to some more wedding-type music. Couples are swishing across the dance floor, and since I don't have a dance partner, I trot over to the cake table.

The woman working the cake table is a serious grump. When I walk up, she acts like she doesn't see me even though I know she totally does. And here's the thing: there are THREE CAKES and none of them are peanut butter flavor. There's a giant, rose-covered, ten-tier white cake for the bride, a big, velvety chocolate airplane for the groom, and a red and blue and brown ice cream cake in the shape of a pheasant (as in, the hunting bird). That one's in honor of the groom's springer spaniel, Seymour.

I stand in front of the big white cake and hold out my plate. The lady hands over a slice. Then I move on to the airplane. When I hold up my plate, she looks at me with these giant bug eyes but finally cuts me off a sliver. *Gee thanks.* Honestly, how many times in my life am I going to get to eat a piece of a cake shaped like an airplane?

"And a slice of the pheasant, *por favor*," I say with a smile to the tight-lipped cake lady. She takes her knife, slices off the bird's butt and plops it onto my plate. I can tell she thinks she's giving me a terrible piece, but it's mostly icing so I couldn't be happier.

I happily clutch my cake trio and scan the room, finally locking eyes with Henry. He's back at our table and he's waving me over. I want to cry happy tears. With the way I ran away from him like that, I wouldn't have been surprised if he'd found a way to switch seats. I wave back and start making my way back to the table when somebody starts clinking their spoon on their water glass. It must be time for speeches.

This should be as fun as watching Granny Malone and her friends play a game of canasta, I think to myself as I lower myself into the seat Prince Henry has thoughtfully pulled out for me. The Archduke of Wincastle, who is at least a hundred years old, goes first. He mumbles something about tradition and prosperity and I don't know what else because, well, it's really boring and I am very busy trying to balance my fork on my water glass. The second he finishes, Penelope bolts out of her seat. She races toward the stage and snatches the mic right out of the archduke's hand.

"What *is* she doing?" Prince Henry whispers to me.

"Thank you, Your Imperial and Royal Highness, for those ever so lovely and inspiring words of wisdom," Penelope gushes. The archduke sits down looking confused. I'm guessing this is not the official order of how things usually go around here.

"Maybe she has a toast for the bride and groom?" I whisper back to Prince Henry. Just as I say this, Penelope glares in my direction and I know she's devised another plan to throw me under a stampede of royal horses.

Penelope clears her throat. "I'd love to offer my best wishes to the bride and groom," she says, looking in their direction. "But I feel it's only right that the next speech be given by the one who wears the Crown Cape. Without further ado, please welcome Princess Wilhelmina of Wincastle!" Penelope smiles, looking oh-so-pleased with herself.

Oh no she didn't!

Every eyeball in the room is on me, including the two that belong to Prince Henry, who looks totally terrified for me. He can't believe I'm actually going to do this and honestly, neither can I. But it's not like I can just run out of the tent or click my heels together and disappear, which would certainly come in handy right about now. I stand up slowly and give Prince Henry a little shrug as I push back my chair. The room starts to spin a little as I walk toward the stage. When I pass Penelope, she bumps me hard in the shoulder and mumbles something I can't make out, thankfully.

I pick up the microphone and scan the crowd of unsmiling, unfamiliar faces. This is almost as bad as the time in third grade when I made it all the way to the Math Olympics and then I froze on the stage and couldn't answer a single question. Actually, it's worse. At least then I didn't have mean old Princess Penelope in the audience, snickering at me and enjoying every second of my humiliation.

"Umm, cheerio everyone," I say, my voice shaking. "I'm sorry, I don't really have anything prepared…" I look over to see Penelope grinning ear to ear, pleased as punch to see me looking like a raccoon caught in headlights. *Not gonna happen, Princess Penny!* I give myself a quick pep talk. *It's now or never, Malone. You've made it this far. You can do this!*

"But I too would like to offer my best wishes to the bride and groom," I start. "Let's give them a nice round of applause!"

Even though I'm clapping like a lunatic, nobody joins in. This is not going well. What can I say about two people I don't even know? *Ooh, I know. Compliments! People love compliments!*

"They sure look fancy today, don't they? I mean, they look perfect—just like a teeny, tiny bride and groom on top of a wedding cake!" I gush, but the crowd just looks confused. I figure that was the wrong thing to say so I try to backpedal. "Except they're not made of cheap plastic and they're definitely not miniature people. In fact they're *huge!*" I say, opening my arms wide. *Hello, they are royalty!* But when I say this, the groom's table lets out a big gasp. Now I realize this is probably because the groom is a little on the hefty side, to say the least. *I'm dead meat.* I seriously want to pick up a fork and dig myself a hole in the grass and climb down into it. *Take a deep breath, Malone. Think,* I tell myself. *Wait, don't think! Just stick to what you know.*

"Starting a brand-new life is a big deal—because you never know what that life is going to be like," I say, and I get a few nods. Man, this is not an easy crowd.

"Princess Clementine and Prince Clayton have it all," I add, and there's lots more nodding and even a few polite grins out there. "But the truth is, their life together won't be perfect. Because no life ever is, even if you're royalty—no disrespect, Your Majesty." I give a quick curtsy toward the queen, who twists her lips into the tiniest of smiles. I kind of expected a little more out of her, after we booty scooted together and all, but whatever. I start to relax a little.

"I'm just a kid, but there's one thing I do know:

Life is like a grab bag from the candy store," I say. "It might be full of the best lollipops you ever tasted, but there's also going to be some horrid, sour jellyfruit in there too." The crowd is chuckling and actually looking happy now, and I'm starting to feel like at least half a million royal bucks.

"So to the bride and groom, I would like to say: May your life together be a lot more sweet than sour, and may every day together be an exciting new adventure!"

I raise my water glass and the whole room goes crazy clapping and cheering. Except for Penelope, who stands and rushes from her seat in a red-faced fury.

Chapter 19

When I Save My MMBs

"Nicely done," Prince Henry says as soon as I get back to the table.

"Thanks," I say, blushing. "Would you excuse me for just a few minutes?"

"Of course," he says, standing with a smile. "Just try to steer clear of that horrible cousin of yours."

I smile back but say nothing. There's no way I'm losing my MMBs over this girl's bratty behavior. *I can do this. I can be the bigger person.*

They've actually built a bathroom out here just for the royal reception. A lady in an apron opens the door for me, and right away I can hear Penelope sobbing inside one of the stalls.

I knock softly on the door.

"Go away," she shouts through her heaving sobs.

"It's me, Mimi," I tell her, mostly because I don't know what else to say.

"Well fluttering fiddlesticks then, *most definitely* go away," Penelope blubbers.

"I'll go away," I say calmly, "when you tell me exactly why it is that you hate me so much."

Penelope whips the door open and stands there glaring at me. Man, is she a mess. Her eyes are all bloodshot and her face looks like a blotchy tomato and she has snot running out of both nostrils. If I had a hankie, I'd give it her, but she'd probably shove it up *my* nose. I close my eyes for a second because I'm afraid she's going to punch me in the face.

"Are you off your blooming trolley?" she howls at me. "You want to know why I hate you so much? Really? You want to know why I, the most unpopular princess Wincastle has ever known, hate you, the most admired and beloved noble in our country's history?"

I assume this is one of those questions you're not supposed to answer, but Penelope is looking at me like she wants me to say something.

"Um, yeah, I guess I do," I say.

"Because you...have...*everything*," she replies, slumping down the wall of the stall and landing in a puddle on the floor. Her sobs grow louder, and I'm starting to worry she's going to choke on her own snot. *Eww.*

"Everyone loves you," she wails. "And not just in Wincastle, but all over the world! You always get all of the attention, and even when I try to mess it up, you come out smelling like a rose. But that's not the worst of it. The worst is that you can't even be bothered to fight back anymore. You used to—you'd get down-right wicked, and when you did, I could tell myself that you were no better than me. But you *are* better than me. You are. Everyone's always known it and I guess I have to face it now too. It's not fair. I hate you and I want to *be* you all at the same time. It's maddening, I tell you. Utterly, spectacularly *maddening*!" She drops her head onto her knees.

"Penelope?" I say it like a question, because I'm not sure if she's going to let me talk.

"What?" she sighs from her spot on the floor.

"You do know that being—wicked, as you say—is a

choice, right?" I ask. "I mean, you could make a decision *right now* that you're only going to say and do nice things. Every day, to everyone. It's really not that complicated."

Penelope lifts her head. "That's easy to say when your life is perfect," she whimpers.

"But how do you know my life is perfect?" I ask. "And what's so bad about yours?"

"Everyone hates me," she sighs. "And it's too late to change that. I'm a lost cause."

"That's not true," I tell her, pulling her to her feet. I push her toward the sink and hand her a wet towel.

"Come on," I say. "We've got to clean you up and get back out there."

"Look at me!" Penelope cries at her reflection in the mirror. "I'm an absolute wreck."

I twist her to face me and dry her eyes with a hand towel. Then I take out the compact that Amelia stashed in my bag. It's tucked in right next to my genie pocket mirror. That reminds me that I'm going to have to tell Frank that he was right. Again. I powder Penelope's nose for her, smooth her hair down, and spin her back around.

"Look, you're beautiful," I tell her.

Our eyes meet in the mirror and she gives me a weak smile. "See?" she says. "And you really are disgustingly kind. I can't believe I never saw that before."

"You're welcome," I say, grabbing her hand and dragging her out the door.

"Where are we going?" Penelope asks as we snake our way through the crowded tent.

"You'll see," I say over my shoulder, squeezing her hand.

We arrive at the wedding party table still holding hands. Prince Henry sees us first and gives me a confused look.

"Prince Henry, I need to rest my feet for a bit, but Princess Penelope was just saying how much she'd fancy a dance with a handsome prince," I say.

Henry is too much of a gentleman to do anything but smile politely and extend his hand to Penelope.

"May I have this dance, Princess?" he asks.

"Oh and Penelope, would you do me a huge favor?" I add. "It's dreadfully hot in this cape, but you know the rules—it must be worn at all times when it's not in its case at the abbey. Would you mind wearing it for a bit? I'd be most grateful." Well, Frank did say I had to make a positive change in this life. Why stop when you're on a roll?

Penelope's jaw drops. "As you wish, Princess Mimi," she says, accepting the cape, which Henry fastens for her. As they make their way toward the dance floor, a hum takes over the room. Flashbulbs start popping wildly again and echoes of *Do you see who is wearing the Crown Cape?* can be heard throughout the tent.

My molasses-stained butt and I sure hope she remembers to bring that thing back, or I'll be sitting here all night.

Chapter 20

When I Find Out What I Didn't Know

As the night wears on, all eyes are on Penelope. She's actually glowing. I don't think it's the Crown Cape either. You can tell she's really happy and having a great time and feeling good about herself. The photographers can't get enough of her. They go wild getting shots of her smiling and dancing in the arms of Prince Henry.

Finally, the party seems to be winding down. At what has to be the stroke of midnight—I'm so tired I'm actually holding my eyelids open with my hands—Penelope flutters back to where I'm sitting and plops down with an exhausted but giddy smile.

"Sorry I was out there so long, Mimi," Penelope says, and you can tell she actually means it. "I just didn't want this night to end. I *still* don't want it to end." Her smile falls a little bit. "But I know it has to, and before it does, there's something I have to tell you."

She bites her bottom lip but says nothing.

"Go on," I tell her. "What is it?" The last of the guests are gathering their things as the service staff bustles around clearing glasses and plates.

Penelope is fiddling with the small evening bag in her lap. She can't even look me in the eye.

"For heaven's sake, Penelope, we're not getting any younger here," I say. "Spit it out already!"

She pops open the clasp on her bag, reaches into it, and pulls out something sparkly.

"I'm so sorry," she whispers, handing it to me. Tears begin spilling down her face.

"What is it?" I ask. "Why are you sorry? I'm so confused!" It's just a pin, sort of like something Granny Flannery always wears on her jacket to church, only this one is ginormous. It has one blue stone the size of a golf ball in the middle and clear sparkly stones— those are only the size of grapes—all around it. They can't be diamonds, surely, or this thing would cost about sixteen trillion dollars.

"Of course you know what it is," Penelope insists. "It's the Berisford-Boyle Brooch, the most important jewel in the entire royal collection! It originally belonged to Queen Millicent's great-great-grandfather, King Winston the Wise. It lives on the Crown Cape, of course." Penelope starts really crying now. "King Winston once had a man's fingers chopped off for *touching* it. And I didn't just touch it; I took it off the Crown Cape and *stole* it."

"But why?" I ask.

"I was going to put it back," Penelope wails. "But later, secretly, after *you'd* been blamed for losing it."

My chin hits the floor.

"Seriously?" I ask, because somebody has to. "Did you graduate from the Ultimate Mean Girl Academy or something? How do you come up with this stuff?"

"I know," Penelope says. "I'm a horrible, horrible person, and I don't blame you if you hate me."

I take Penelope's hands in mine. "I don't hate you," I tell her. "You acted like a jerk and I might hate what you did, but I don't hate you. We're cousins, for crying out loud. But if you keep saying that you're a horrible person, pretty soon you're going to start believing it and turn into a horrible person, and that would be a serious shame."

Penelope smiles. I give her a big hug and she hugs me back tightly so I know she means it and I'm glad. I can't stand those pat-pat-pat fake hugs some people give. I say if you don't act like you're trying to squeeze the breath out of the other person, you're doing it wrong.

Just then I see Amelia making her way toward us.

"Hurry," I tell Penelope. "Help me get this thing back onto the Crown Cape!"

Penelope slips the pin into position just as Amelia reaches our table.

"Good evening, ladies," she says. "I trust you had an enjoyable time?"

Penelope and I nod and squeeze hands.

"It certainly looked like it," Amelia adds. "Quite lovely to see the two of you looking like…friends. But it is time to go."

"Good night, Princess Mimi," Penelope says, giving me another of those award-winning hugs. "Thank you…for everything."

"Night, Penelope," I say, squeezing with all of my might. *Don't mess this up*, I add silently.

"That was quite a lovely thing you did back there, Princess," Amelia says as we cross the lawn together. "You may have actually put an end to years of bitterness between your families with your generosity of spirit."

"It was nothing. Really, I just..." I begin, but Amelia keeps talking.

"Ever since that horrible newspaper printed those photographs of you two leaving the hospital the very same week with your families," Amelia says, shaking her head, "naming you the most beautiful princess in all Christendom and Penelope the ugliest. It's been really hard for her."

"But she *is* beautiful!" I protest.

"Yes, she is, but she never thought so, and she became what had been said of her," Amelia says as we arrive at my door. "That may have all changed tonight. You did a good thing tonight, Princess, a very good thing indeed." Amelia kisses me on the forehead and tells me good night.

Huh, I think to myself. So that's what happened. *You don't know what you don't know until you do.*

I'm so sleepy as I step out of my big fat baby dress and lay it across the chair in my room. I brush my teeth, at least a little, and it takes all the strength I have left to climb up into that crazy tall princess bed.

* * *

Ugh! Who is rubbing my face with sandpaper? I wake up eyeball to eyeball with my cat Charlotte, who is licking my cheeks like it's her job or something.

I sit up in bed, rubbing my eyes and giving Charlotte a squeeze around the middle, which sends her leaping for the door. There's my polka-dot chair in the corner, and my zebra-striped rug and the purple vanity table that I helped my mom paint. The dusty old MMBs are propped up next to the vanity. I'm back at home, back to being Maggie Malone, just like that.

The phone rings. It's Stella.

"What are you doing *right now*?" she booms into my ear.

"Uh… waking up… I think," I say.

"Well, I'm on my way over," Stella pants. It sounds like she's jogging. "Celebrity Times just posted pictures from the royal wedding and there's this big deal about the Crown Cloak—I'll explain when I get to your house!"

"It's the Crown Cape," I mutter, but she's already hung up the phone.

I jump out of bed, throw on some shorts and a T-shirt, and pull up the Celebrity Times home page. Smack in the middle is the most elegant photograph of Princess Penelope smiling as she's being swung around by Prince Henry. The Crown Cape is swirling behind her beneath the headline, "The Swan of Wincastle: Say Hello to Princess Penelope!"

"Forget Princess Mimi!" Stella announces, shutting my door behind her. "It's all about Princess Penelope now. Apparently, Princess Mimi has been hogging the spotlight all these years, trying to keep poor Penelope from getting any attention because look how gorgeous she is!" Stella says, pointing to the image of Princess Penelope on my computer.

"Really? How do you know that's what happened?" I ask, trying my best to seem clueless.

"That's what all the royal websites are saying. Anyway, Princess Penelope is pretty much the *chosen princess* now, and she's probably going to marry Prince Henry when they're old enough," Stella moans. "Just look at them in this picture—they're so crushing on each other!"

"You think?" I ask, pretending to inspect the picture closely. "Well, maybe…"

I change the subject. "Hey, I'm starving! Want to go get some doughnuts?"

"Does a one-legged duck swim in a circle?" Stella answers, slinging one arm around my shoulders as we head for the door.

"Dippin' Donuts here we come! I hope we're not too late for double doozie chocolate doughnuts!" I say, popping the kickstand on my bike and hopping on. Stella and I can't figure out why they don't just make more of those, since they always run out.

Stella swings the big glass door open for me.

"I'm desperate for the loo!" I say without thinking.

"You're desperate for who?" Stella asks, confused. "Who the heck is Lou? Is he some hottie at Pinkerton?"

"Uh…no! I mean, what?" I say. "I just meant I've got to go to the bathroom before I order!"

"Yeah? So why are you talking about some dude if you've got to hit the stall?"

Did I mention Stella doesn't let things go as well as I do?

"Oh! Loo is British slang for bathroom," I explain. "I was watching this…"

"Yeah, yeah, just hurry, Malone," Stella says. "It looks like there are only four double-doozies left."

What I meant was that Stella doesn't let things go until she's bored of them.

Chapter 21

When the Handmaidens Start to Break Down

Before I know it, it's Monday morning. When I was at Sacred Heart, we always started the first hour of the week with a school sing-along. It might sound corny, but it was actually really fun, and it made everyone excited to come back to school, even if you'd had the best weekend ever. There's no Monday love at Pinkerton, even on a good week. And this is definitely not a good week, especially if you're a handmaiden. So you can see why I'm taking my sweet time getting to school today.

I pull up to the bike rack at the same time as Elizabeth.

"What's up, buttercup?" I ask Elizabeth, unsnapping my bike helmet and hanging it on the handlebar of my bike.

Elizabeth mutters something I can't really make out. She's fishing around in her backpack and looking like she's about to panic.

"What's wrong, Elizabeth?" I ask, but now she looks like she's having a full-on, freak-out attack.

"I can't FIND it!" Elizabeth screams. Now *that* I heard.

"Whoa. Way to turn up the volume there, Lizzie! Whatcha looking for? Can I help?" I ask.

"Uh-uh…I thought I put it in here last night, but maybe I…oh no…" she trails off.

"And what was *it*, again?" I ask, thinking *it* must be a live hamster she's afraid she crushed with her math book. Poor little guy.

"Lucy asked me to reserve a bike rack space for her on the end and so my mom took me to the Pet Palace and I had a silver, diamond-bedazzled tag engraved with her name on it with a chain that I could hang across the space and now it's GONE!" Elizabeth's face is the color of a fire engine, and I think she's about to actually start wailing. In fact, I think I can hear the sirens warming up.

"Wow," I say, "That's really…wow! Well, I'm sure

she'll understand." I don't point out to her that Lucy might take offense at the dog suggestion.

"No!" Elizabeth screams, again with plenty of volume and this time with crazy eyes. "You go on to homeroom—it's all my fault—I'll stay here and guard her spot till the bell rings in case Lucy decided to ride her bike today. I'm fine—really!"

But I can tell Elizabeth is not even close to fine. I think the stress of being somebody's handmaiden is starting to wear on her. I get it, I guess. Lucy can be seriously mean when things don't go her way. The other day, she asked Alicia to bring her jean skirt to school so she could wear it—the one with the hot pink ruffle around the bottom. Alicia misunderstood and brought her jean skirt with the star-shaped, leopard pockets instead. Lucy was furious and made Alicia wear the thing *backwards* all day. Alicia acted like it was an inside "handmaiden joke" and pretended not to care, but I know she did. How could she *not* care? It looked ridiculous—all pouchy in the front—plus all day long, kids kept pointing it out. "Hey, Alicia, you've got your skirt on backwards!" Mr. Mooney almost gave her a detention for inappropriate dress, until Lucy swooped in at the last possible second and saved her. *What a great friend.*

"Okay, I'll see you in homeroom," I tell Elizabeth, because I can tell she's fully committed to taking a late slip over a bike rack slot that Lucy *may or may not* need. She's probably afraid Lucy will make her wear that dog collar around her neck if she doesn't follow through on her orders.

Chimichanga! How did things get so out of control? I wonder, shaking my head. Back in Wincastle, I probably could have figured a way out of this ridiculous mess, but I don't have a clue how to stop the madness in my own life.

"Where's Elizabeth?" Alicia asks just as I take my seat.

"Um, I think she's guarding Lucy's possible parking spot in the bike rack outside," I say, lifting my eyebrows just a little so she knows I think that's pretty nutty.

"Well, she better get in here, and fast," Alicia whispers. "Lucy has an announcement."

Uh-oh, I think to myself. I'm no psychic, but I'm pretty sure this can't be good.

Chapter 22

When I Start to Put the Pieces Together

Mrs. Richter is a good five minutes into morning announcements when Elizabeth slinks in with her late slip.

"Please take your seat, Elizabeth," Mrs. Richter says. Right then Lucy raises her hand.

"Yes, Lucy?" Mrs. Richter asks.

"I'd like to make an announcement, if that's okay," Lucy says sweetly. Mrs. Richter doesn't look so sure about this, but like everybody else, she's terrified of Mr. Mooney when it comes to anything involving the royal court.

"Please be quick, Lucy," Mrs. Richter sighs, taking a seat behind her big, beat-up desk.

Lucy flounces to the front of the room.

"Good morning, everyone," she says, adjusting her princess apprentice sash. She hasn't been seen without that thing since the day she was appointed. I'll bet she wears it to bed. "As you know, there are only a few weeks left before the Pinkerton Royal Ball and the crowning of the actual Pinkerton Prince and Princess." Lucy claps her hands frantically, glancing around, encouraging the applause. A few people half-heartedly join in, probably out of fear. "Anyway, I've been speaking to Mr. Mooney about some, well, *problems* the apprentices have been having with some of our handmaidens." She looks right at Elizabeth here, and poor Elizabeth slumps down in her seat. Her face starts to get that splotchy-red look that means she's probably going to cry. Lucy smiles—one of those mean smiles that send shivers up your neck—and continues. "And Mr. Mooney agreed that the apprentices should be allowed to replace their handmaidens at any time, you know, so that we can maintain the *integrity* of the Royal Court. So I just wanted to let everyone know that I will most likely be appointing at least one new handmaiden this week," and here she looks at me and then Alicia. "Possibly two or even three. So, good luck everyone! And remember, I'm watching you."

Lucy gives the class this exaggerated wink and then prances back to her seat, looking pretty pleased with herself. I can't even look at Elizabeth. I just can't.

"Well, thank you, Lucy, for that *very interesting* announcement," Mrs. Richter says. I am almost positive I see her roll her eyes just a tiny bit.

Mrs. Richter starts going on and on about state testing and some visit by the Distinguished Schools Committee, but I am so angry that I can't even take in a word she's saying. *Lucy St. Claire, you've gone too far this time*, I think to myself, wondering if there is actual steam coming out of my ears. *You must have gone through the line five times the day they were handing out nerve. For the love of black licorice bits, Elizabeth bought you a bedazzled, personalized bike-spot holder! And Alicia brought you fresh, gluten-free blueberry muffins every single day last week, and I've lost track of how many Cokes I've bought you from that vending machine. Maybe Elizabeth and Alicia are willing to keep putting up with your demanding, backstabbing ways but I, Maggie Malone, have had enough.*

I raise my hand and ask to be excused. Mrs. Richter hands me the giant yellow paddle you have to carry when you're in the halls during class, to show that you've gotten permission to be wandering around and aren't planning to skip across the street to Burger Barn for a vanilla shake. I take the paddle and head out the door, making a beeline for the nearest bathroom.

"Frank!" I whisper, after I've checked under all of the stalls and made sure there are no feet.

This time he appears immediately. He's sitting at a big metal desk with several stacks of papers in front of him and a pencil tucked behind his ear.

"Malone," he says. "I figured I'd be hearing from you again today. Pardon the mess. It's bookkeeping day."

I'm about to ask him why genies have to do paperwork—I mean, what good is *magic* if you can't wiggle your ears and have boring stuff like that just taken care of?—but then I remember that I'm in the middle of a major crisis here.

"Frank, this whole handmaiden thing has to stop," I tell him. "I mean, seriously. It's out of control. And please don't tell me that 'I've got this' again, because I don't even know what that means."

"How did you handle Princess Penelope?" Frank sighs, shuffling through one of the piles of papers as if he's looking for something specific.

"I was just *nice* to her!" I practically shout. "I don't really think that's going to work with Lucifer here."

"It wasn't *just* that you were nice to her, Malone," Frank tells me, slamming a stapler into a thick stack of papers. The sharp bang makes me jump. "You gave her something that she needed all along. What do you think this Lucifer—uh, Lucy—really needs?"

"A personality transplant?" I say, only half joking.

"Remember, Malone, you can't change anybody else but you *can* change how you react to them," Frank says. Just when I'm about to ask him for the seventy-seven-hundredth time what in the spinning universe *that* means, an eighth grade girl strolls into the bathroom and into one of the stalls. The whole room echoes when she slams the door.

"You've got this," Frank mouths silently, fading out.

I've got this, I repeat, not because I believe it, but because I don't.

Chapter 23

When I Accidentally Inspire a Handmaiden Uprising

I go back to class and try to settle in and listen to what Mrs. Richter is saying, but I'm so mad all my ears can hear is "Wah, wah, wah, wah, wah…" above the blood boiling in my brain. Seriously. What in the world could make Lucy want to be that nasty? She's planning on *firing* us? *I don't think so.* Not if I can shake some sense into my fellow handmaidens first.

It's all I can do to sit through three more classes before lunch. At the end of Spanish class, I slip Elizabeth and Alicia notes asking them to meet me in the MPR by the stage. I give them the option to check the yes or no box and they both check yes.

I've been sitting on the end of the stage waiting for a

couple of minutes when Elizabeth and Alicia stroll in, letting the door slam behind them.

"Easy there, girls!" I say. "This is a secret hand-maiden meeting!"

"Wait, what if Lucy catches us planning official handmaiden business without her?" Elizabeth asks, and I swear the kid is acting like a puppy that's been spanked on the behind way too many times. Like, if she had a tail, it would definitely be tucked between her legs.

"Okay, see?" I point out. "That's the problem right there! You don't even think you can talk to your two *real friends* without checking it out with Lucifer first."

Alicia and Elizabeth both gasp and take a big step back from me.

"That's right, I said it!" I say, hopping off the stage, waving my arms and flashing my hands. "Because— *hello*—it's the truth! Lucy St. Claire is as mean as the devil! I bet she keeps a pitchfork in her locker, which is probably full of hot ashes!"

Alicia and Elizabeth are shaking their heads and have both turned as pale as Duane, the blind albino guinea pig Stella used to have. That girl has some pretty bad pet luck. Whenever she used to let little Duane out of his cage, he would run around like he was on fire everywhere he went and was always bonking his head into doorways and chair legs. Still, Stella loved that ugly little rodent, which I think says something about the sort of person she is.

"That's right, girls!" I say, throwing my hands on my hips. "I'll say it again. Our noble little Lucifer is the meanest, worst princess apprentice ever, and I, for one, am not going to take her ridiculously rude treatment anymore. Now who's with me?"

Alicia and Elizabeth say nothing. In fact, they're not even really looking at me, but sort of *past me.*

"Hello?" I shout. "Anyone home?"

Alicia lifts her arm, really slowly, and points toward the back of the stage.

I glance over my shoulder.

Double-decker disaster.

It turns out Alicia and Elizabeth weren't outraged by what I was saying as much as they were petrified by the sight of Lucy standing on the stage right behind me—along with her tagalong serf sidekick, Winnie, of course.

"That's it!" Lucy spits with a loud stomp that echoes across the MPR. *Did she just use her pitchfork to make that kind of noise?*

"You three have given me no choice. You're *all* fired—every last one of you. I was planning to keep a couple of you on for a day or two longer to train the new handmaidens," Lucy says, motioning to three sixth grade girls cowering at the corner of the stage.

How'd *they* get in here?

"You know, to make your trip back to *Nobodyville* a little less embarrassing. But I can't do that now, can I?" Lucy says with an evil grin and sideways squinty eyes.

Look out, people, she's not even pretending to be fake-nice anymore.

"Maggie's right!" booms Elizabeth, loud enough that I think it probably rocked Mr. Mooney's desk in his office across the school. The girl has definitely found her voice.

"You're totally mean and for no good reason!" Elizabeth continues.

Apparently Elizabeth and Alicia have been as fed up as I have—they just needed a little help saying it out loud. Alicia even throws in a little twist of her own.

"And actually we had a supersecret handmaiden meeting *before* this fake handmaiden meeting," Alicia chimes in. "We quit being your handmaidens at least ten minutes ago so you *can't* fire us! You can fire Winnie, if you want to fire somebody!"

Winnie is terrified, looking around, shifting left to right. Even Lucy looks confused, like she's not sure what her next move should be. That's a first. Just then, Elizabeth—the same girl who before today barely spoke above a whisper—pipes up again and quashes the whole handmaiden nonsense once and for all.

"Hey, you guys," Elizabeth calls over to the shaky sixth grader handmaidens-in-waiting. "Do you like being yelled at, humiliated, ordered around, and never—I mean ever—getting a thank-you for anything you do?"

The kid's really on a roll.

"If you do, you're going to *love* being Lucy's minion, I mean *handmaiden*," she says, walking over to the girls in the corner.

"You know what, Lucy?" one of the girls says shyly. "I forgot that I have, um, a thing after school…"

"Yeah, I definitely have a thing too, so you know, maybe you should find some other handmaidens…" says a second.

"Now look what you've done!" Lucy shouts, marching up to Elizabeth until they are eyeball to eyeball. Elizabeth doesn't flinch, and I silently cheer for her. "Who do you think you are?"

The not-minions scamper out the back door by the stage.

"I don't really know," Elizabeth says, her voice shaking a tiny bit but still loud and clear. "But I know I'm not anybody's *handmaiden*."

"Come on, Winnie!" Lucy huffs, dragging Winnie by the shirtsleeve through the MPR and right out the double doors.

"Did that really just happen?" Elizabeth asks, looking like she's in shock.

"It totally did," I tell her, putting my arm around her. "How great do you feel?"

"Really great," Elizabeth says, linking her arm with mine. "And also? I'm starving!"

"Me too," Alicia says, falling in on the other side.

"What do you say we get ourselves some lunch?" I say, laughing. "And maybe even sit down to eat it! We are handmaidens no more!"

Chapter 24

When Lucy Puts Down Her Pitchfork

Word about the Great Handmaiden Rebellion—that's actually what kids are calling it—spreads across Pinkerton like one of those famous California wildfires. And try as she might, Lucy can't seem to get anyone else on the entire campus to accept the "honor" of being her servant. Except poor Winnie, of course. That girl is probably at home right now ironing Lucy's underpants or organizing her multiplication flash cards.

"Way to stand up to Lucifer," a super-popular seventh grader whispers to me in the library before school. I've got a massive poetry project due next week and the whole handmaiden business put me a bit behind. Did you know that poetry doesn't even have to *rhyme*? I just learned that this week. It sort of threw me for a loop. How is it even poetry if it doesn't rhyme? Even if it *is* poetry, I like the rhyming kind way better.

"Yeah, good for you," her friend adds. "That whole handmaiden thing was pretty stupid."

"Thanks, you guys," I say with a smile, turning back to my page full of perfectly rhyming sentences.

The first warning bell rings and I start packing up my stuff. Just as I'm sliding *The Greatest Poetry of All Time*—a title that I'm thinking might be a bit of a stretch—back onto a shelf, I spot Lucy sitting at a table on the other side of the library, all alone. She must feel my eyes on her, because right then she looks up and our eyes meet. She doesn't give me her famous evil glare or start screaming at me and calling me names, which for a scary, heart-stopping minute, I think she might do. She looks so sad I almost want to say something to her, but I have to get to homeroom. I'm one late slip away from detention as it is, and I'm pretty sure my mom's head would spin right off her neck if I came home with *that* bit of good news.

"Have you seen Lucy today?" Elizabeth whispers, taking the seat right behind me in homeroom.

"I just did, in the library," I whisper back. "She looks *awful*, like somebody just flushed her goldfish down the toilet or something."

"I know," Elizabeth says. "I wonder what's up. Do you think it's all of the handmaiden stuff?"

I don't have time to answer because the final bell rings then, and Lucy walks through the door just in the nick of time. I notice that for the first time since she was appointed, she's not even wearing her princess apprentice sash. But that's not even the weirdest thing. Instead of standing over some random person and demanding *her seat*—which I've learned since I got here changes almost daily—she shuffles to the very back of the classroom and sits down without causing even a minor scene.

I hope this isn't the old calm before the storm, I think to myself. Then I try to forget about Lucy St. Claire and focus instead on how nice it is *not* being anybody's handmaiden.

Chapter 25

When I Take Lucy for a Ride

I'm working my bike lock combination and thinking about the banana sandwich I'm going to make the second I get home when I hear this crazy commotion in the car pickup line. Somebody is banging on their horn like they've got a drum solo in a parade and screaming like a banshee. I'm not exactly sure what a banshee is, but my dad's always given me the impression that they're famous for yelling their heads off.

I quit messing with my lock and stroll over to see what's going on.

"I *mean* it," a girl is shouting from a beat-up blue station wagon. "You have exactly fifteen seconds to get your annoying face into this car or I am leaving you here, do you hear me?"

"I'll be right there, Libby," a voice shouts from the crowd of kids who have gathered. "I forgot my science folder and I have a paper due tomorrow, so I need it. Give me two minutes!" I find the face that's attached to the voice. It's Lucy, and she's looking pretty frantic.

"I'll give you *nothing*," the Libby person bellows, laying on the horn again. She's the fourth or fifth car in the line and obviously not happy about it. "Just as soon as I can move this car, I'm out of here! I told you, if you're not ready when I come to get you, you can walk home!"

"Libby, please, wait!" Lucy pleads. "It'll take me an hour to walk home, and Mom will kill me because I won't have time to do my chores. I'll hurry!"

"Not! My! Problem! Peon!" Libby shouts between honks, revving the gas pedal with her foot.

Lucy races up the stairs and I stand there, wishing there was something I could do. I know, Lucy treated me worse than a speck of dirt on a flea on a tick on a rat, but from the looks of this sister of hers, it's probably all she knows. Lucy is back in way less than two minutes—in just enough time to see Libby make it to the front of the line and then gun her car right out of the parking lot in a smoky cloud of gravel.

Lucy sits down on the stairs and puts her head in her hands. I'm not even sure why myself, but I walk over and sit down next to her.

"Your sister seems really sweet," I say. Lucy looks up and half-laughs.

"Yeah, she's a little sliver of chocolate cream pie, that one," she says, wiping at her eyes.

"Where do you live?" I ask her.

"Over on the west side," Lucy says.

"On Windham Hill?" I ask. That's the fancy part of town where the houses look like castles and you get a country club membership just for living there.

"No, not anymore," Lucy says, sniffling. "I live in one of those apartments over behind the mall now."

"The ones that have the giant pool with the super-high diving board you can see from the food court?" I ask.

"Those are the ones," Lucy says, obviously not as impressed as I am by that diving board.

"Maybe you could take the bus?" I suggest. "I know for a fact that it goes right by there."

"It's just, well, I've never taken the bus before," Lucy admits, looking embarrassed and a little scared. "My parents used to have somebody pick me up."

"Well I'm a pro," I tell her. "My dad thinks every kid should know how to get around on her own, so I've ridden that thing all over town. I could even go with you. You know, to make sure you get home okay. They have a bike rack right on the front of the bus."

"Why would you do that for me?" Lucy asks, looking more than a little surprised.

"Why not?" I say. "I'd want somebody to do it for me if it was my first time!"

"That's really nice of you, Maggie," she says. "Thanks."

By the time we both get all of our stuff together, Pinkerton is practically a ghost town, but the stragglers who remain stare us down, looking pretty confused. I'm guessing they think Lucy is going to unhinge her jaw and swallow me whole, like one of those big snakes you see on the Jungle Channel. But I really don't think she will. I think she's more like a toothless piranha—you know those tiny fish down in South America that swim in lakes and look perfectly harmless until they open their mouths and you see their ginormous set of choppers. I saw a MeTube video of a pile of those little guys gobble up a deer in about thirty seconds. I really wish I could unsee that.

I walk my bike alongside Lucy down the sidewalk to the bus stop.

"Here we are," I say, propping my bike against the metal shelter and scrolling down with my finger until I find our bus route.

"And it looks like the bus should be here in about five minutes," I add, checking my watch. "We just made it."

"I always thought this was just a rain shed," Lucy says, looking around. "You know, for people to get out of the rain?"

"Um, yeah, well, it's good for that when they're waiting for the bus," I say, realizing that this kid's got no street smarts at all.

Our bus comes and the driver is so sweet, he hops right off the bus with a smile and lifts my bike onto the rack for me.

"Thank you, kind sir!" I say, with a fake British accent that doesn't sound anything like Princess Mimi. Well, you can't blame a girl for trying.

I pay for both our fares since it's only a couple of bucks and then walk Lucy over to a pair of empty, forward-facing seats. I don't know if she's a kid who gets carsick, so I'm not taking any chances with the sideways seating.

"So this is the bus," I say, looking around at a guy in a business suit reading the paper, a woman in a Burger Barn uniform, and a teenage boy who probably goes to Franklin High, if I had to guess. "It's great and it'll take you just about anywhere you need to go," I say.

"You know, we just moved into an apartment," Lucy tells me.

"Yeah, you mentioned the ones behind the mall?" I ask, not thinking too much about what she's just said. "Those look pretty cool. And honestly, I've had dreams about that diving board! Is it awesome?"

"My whole family," Lucy continues, ignoring my very important diving board question. "We're squished into a two bedroom with one tiny plastic shower and hot water that only works for about fifteen minutes. So of course Libby always takes the first shower."

"Oh, well that's…" I try to chime in, but I realize Lucy isn't done.

"You heard about my dad's company—well, really my grandfather's company that my dad was in charge of—it went out of business," Lucy says, looking down.

"Oh no, I didn't know that," I say.

"Yeah," Lucy continues. "The bank sold our house on the courthouse steps—which I don't really get because it never moved from where it's always been."

"I think that's a term they use for..." I try to interject, but it's no use.

"It all happened a few months ago, right before Libby's sweet sixteen party where one of Becca Starr's backup singers was supposed to perform," Lucy explains. "Of course that all got canceled and some people even said my dad might go to jail for bamboozling money or something like that."

"I'm so sorry, Lucy," I finally say. "I had no idea."

"Yeah," she says, staring off. "You're pretty new at Pinkerton so you might not know this, but I was the girl who had the biggest birthday parties and gave the best goody bags ever. Like, for my tenth birthday party, my mom rented out Spa Serene—the whole entire place—and every girl at my party got mani-pedis, massages, *and* facials. And the goody bags were sequin purses with real rhinestone tiaras in them."

"Wow, that's really..." I say, trying to find the right words. For my tenth birthday, we bobbed for apples and had a three-legged race, and the gift bags were brown paper lunch bags—Stella and I painted everyone's names on them and they came out really cute—with plastic rainbow Slinkies and a Bubble Pop inside. "That's, just, wow."

"Yeah, well, now I'm sure no one's ever going to want to be my friend because what are they going to get out of it?"

Okay, that's officially the saddest thing I've ever heard. And from Lucy St. Claire. I think my heart is about to crack open, I feel so bad for her. Not because she lives in a cramped apartment, or because her dad lost his company, but because she thinks she has to pass out presents to get friends. Then I realize something.

"Is that why you came up with the handmaiden thing?" I ask her. "To get friends?"

"Well, I guess I figured you guys would *have* to be my friends if it was official royal business," Lucy explains, looking at her feet.

"Really?" I ask, and then I wish I could take it back. Lucy's face turns really red and she looks out the bus window.

"I know, it was a pretty bad plan," she says. "But as soon as we lost all of our money, my two supposedly best friends—Kat Witherspoon and Remi Reynolds—dropped me like a dirty diaper. I didn't know what else to do…"

Lucy trails off, and of course I think about Stella. My best friend might think she knows everything about everything and sometimes she drives me nuts when she sings her made-up song lyrics over the real ones so I can't hear them, but she's as loyal as any dog you ever met. Stella wouldn't care if I lived in a tent or had to Dumpster-dive for my lunch. Because, really, what did that have to do with anything?

"Well, I'm sorry about Kat and Remi," I tell her. "That stinks."

Lucy nods.

"Ooh, your stop is next," I tell her.

Lucy starts gathering her stuff.

"You probably have other plans, but if not, would you want to come over this weekend for a swim?" she says, not looking at me. "I mean, Libby will probably be there, and you already got a glimpse of *that*, but I could make us some lunch and stuff and maybe she'll be off with her boyfriend or at the mall or something…"

"Are fish waterproof?" I ask her.

"Oh," Lucy says. "Well, maybe some other time then."

"Sorry," I laugh. "That means yes. I'd love to come over for a swim!"

"Cool," she says, looking relieved. "Thanks again, Maggie. You know, for helping me get home. And for not making fun of me or anything…and for giving me another chance."

"You're totally welcome," I tell Lucy St. Claire, who might just turn out to be not so royally horrible after all.

Chapter 26

When It's Back to Doughnuts for Me

"Well?" Stella demands, throwing my bedroom door open with a bang and scaring me so badly I knock over the card house I've been building for the last thirty minutes.

"Jeez, Stella, you sure know how to make an entrance," I laugh, catching my breath and scooping up the cards.

Stella plops down on my bed and pushes a bag toward me.

"I stopped at Dippin' Donuts on the way here," she says, out of breath. "Got the last two double doozie chocolate doughnuts!"

"Okay, I forgive you for scaring me half to death," I tell her, pulling out my little ring of heaven and a napkin. My mom doesn't love it when I eat in my room, but as long as I vacuum my zebra rug afterward, she lets me do it without too much fuss.

"Anyway," Stella says dramatically. "How was the big Pinkerton Imperial Princess Festival or whatever it's called?"

"It's called the Pinkerton Royal Ball and it was a blast," I tell her. "This girl in a wheelchair got crowned Pinkerton Princess and everybody was crying and everything."

"Yeah, that sounds like a total blast," Stella says sarcastically.

"Well, there was a band and dancing and really good food too," I tell her.

"And what about that Lucy girl?" Stella wants to know. "Has she jumped back on the crazy train yet?"

"Lucy's okay," I tell Stella. "She just had some stuff to figure out. She actually got up and gave this really awesome speech at the royal ball about how maybe the dukes and princess apprentices aren't such a great idea because they take the spotlight off the prince and princess. I seriously thought Mr. Mooney was going to lose it for a minute, but then she added this part where she thought Mr. Mooney deserved to be called *Sir* Mooney as soon as the royal court was announced—at least until the ball—and he seemed to like that idea a lot. Anyway, Lucy said she's going to run for student council president next year and really shake up the royal court."

"Mother of a baby squirrel monkey, speaking of royal courts, I almost forgot!" Stella shouts, pulling a *Tween Scene* magazine out of her backpack. "Did you hear that Princess Penelope and Prince Henry are officially a couple? It says here they're probably going to get married. I mean, not for like fifteen years or something, but it's pretty much a done deal. And look at them hanging out on the royal yacht," Stella adds, shaking the magazine right in my face. "How lucky can a girl get? Honestly."

A girl can get pretty darned lucky, I think to myself with a smile.

Maggie Malone's Totally Fab Vocab

Just like I love to try out new lives, I also love to try out new words! Here's a list of some sort-of-fancy words I used in this book that you might not have known before. I included a synonym for each, but you could probably figure out what they mean from the way I used them in the story. Now that you know these words, don't be afraid to use them. Being smart is totally cool.

1. Affair: event
2. Amusing: entertaining
3. Appointed: nominated
4. Apprentices: beginners
5. Beam: radiate
6. Bedazzled: decorated

7. Blubbers: cries noisily

8. Bolts: shoots out from; rushes

9. Brooch: decorative pin

10. Canasta: a card game

11. Christendom: all Christians

12. Clasp: lock; fastening

13. Committed: dedicated; unwavering

14. Complicated: confusing

15. Customs: traditions

16. Desperate: in dire need

17. Diorama: a 3-D model

18. Drones: male honeybees

19. Enlightenment: spiritual wisdom

20. Esteemed: admired

21. Flustered: confused; upset

22. Formal: fancy and old-fashioned

23. Fortress: castle

24. Fury: rage; anger

25. Glares: scowls; looks angrily

26. Glimpse: quick look; peek

27. Glory: honor

28. Halfheartedly: not enthusiastically

29. Hefty: large; muscular; solid

30. Hesitates: pauses; waits

31. Humiliation: embarrassment

32. Impression: feeling; sense

33. Inspect: scrutinize; look closely

34. Inspiring: moving; uplifting

35. Installed: put in

36. Lagoons: small ponds

37. Loyal: faithful

38. Media: news outlets

39. Monocle: single eyeglass

40. Mousse: custard

41. Narrowing: getting smaller

42. Peeved: irritated

43. Pitchfork: long handled fork

44. Plastering: spreading

45. Polar: extreme

46. Pooling: coming together

47. Positioned: arranged

48. Positive: good

49. Precisely: exactly

50. Prosperity: wealth

51. Quashes: suppresses

52. Relayed: delivered

53. Revolutionized: transformed
54. Rhinestone: fake diamond
55. Riot: uprising
56. Rodent: pertaining to gnawing, nibbling animals like rats
57. Sarcastically: scornfully
58. Serf: slave
59. Shock: jarring visual
60. Smirk: sly smile
61. Smug: pleased with oneself
62. Sophisticated: cultured
63. Stampede: rush of animals
64. Stashed: hid
65. Stragglers: lingerers
66. Swanky: fancy
67. Taunted: teased
68. Taut: tight
69. Unhinge: open wide
70. Vile: horrible

Take a sneak peek
at the next

Maggie
Malone

adventure!

Maggie Malone Makes a Splash

Coming May 2015

"It's so not fair," I tell my reflection in the mirror. "I'm *not* jealous that Elizabeth is a better swimmer than me! Well maybe I am a little tiny bit, but I never, ever lie! If Elizabeth doesn't quit the swim team, that evil Brianna and her ugly swimsuit will make our lives miserable! What am I going to do? How am I ever going to fix this?"

"Are you asking yourself or me?" Frank says.

"AAAAAAAAAAAACCCCCCCCCCCCCCCC CCKKKKKKKKKKKKKKKKKK!" I scream, tipping over backward in my chair. I land in a heap on my zebra rug, my heart pounding harder than it did that time my brother Mickey and his friend Oliver hid under my bed and waited until I was *this close* to falling asleep before they rolled out, jumped up, and shouted GOTCHA! right into my face. I nearly busted a gut that time. *His.*

"Geez, Frank, could you give a girl some warning before you just show up next time?" I ask, pulling myself back up into my chair.

"If I'm not mistaken, *you* called *me*," Frank-in-the-mirror laughs.

Frank came with my MMBs—Mostly Magical Boots—and the only way I can talk to him is in the mirror. Since I haven't had the MMBs that long, I'm not always sure exactly how it all works. But this is definitely the first time Frank has just shown up like this, practically uninvited. Still, I'm pretty glad to see him. I need *somebody* to talk to.

"Well, since you're here and everything," I tell Frank, "you got any of that great genie advice you're so famous for? Just please don't tell me that I've got this, okay? Because I obviously don't. Like, at all." I let out a huge sigh. My heartbeat is slowing to a normal rhythm again, thankfully.

"Which part of this little mess do you want my help with?" Frank asks.

"Well, I... Wait, what's that clicking sound?" I ask, totally distracted by the noise.

Frank holds up a pair of knitting needles and a huge ball of bright blue yarn. "I'm making a beanie," he says. "What? Knitting relaxes me."

"You're weird," I tell Frank.

"Compared to all the other genies you know?" Frank asks with a laugh, click-clacking away.

"Whatever, I just don't know how to make Elizabeth believe me. Brianna said that if I don't convince Elizabeth to quit the team, she's going to make us pay. Elizabeth is brand-new but totally outswam Brianna during tryouts. She's super jealous!" I explain, resting my chin in my hands.

"I hear you," Frank says, setting his knitting needles aside. "That little whippersnapper's a piece of work. Who peed in her Cheerios anyway?"

"Okay, that's just gross," I say, cringing.

"Here's the thing, Malone," he says, leaning in. "You can't control what other people do...or how they act, what they say, or what they believe. All *you* can do is be yourself. Stay 100% Maggie Malone—you know the deal—in every situation. Now *that's* some excellent genie advice, if I do say so myself." Franks nods, so pleased with himself.

"But that bratty little girl's going to…" I protest.

"Nope!" Frank holds up a hand to stop me.

"And Elizabeth thinks that I…" I plead.

"No ma'am, Pam," Frank says.

"Wait, who's Pam?" I ask, confused.

"That's just something people say, you know like 'hop on the bus, Gus,' or 'slip out the back, Jack,' or…" Frank continues.

"What?" I ask because honestly, genies can be so confusing. "Not to be selfish, but I really don't care about your friends Pam or Gus or Jack right now. As a matter of fact, all I really want to do is crawl under a rock and wait for all this to be over. Or sink deep down to the ocean floor, far away from this mess where the only things I can hear are dolphins and waves and OH MY GOSH THAT'S IT!"

"WHAT'S IT?" Frank looks up because apparently he'd gone back to his beanie.

"Marina Tide! I want to be her!" I explain, jumping up, throwing my hands over my head. "She lives down in Florida…well technically, she lives wherever her big boat takes her, but she's off the coast of sunny Florida right now and it's freezing here so...I'll soak up the sun and swim with Skipper and probably save a coral reef! It's going to be amazing!"

"Sounds like a plan, Stan!" Frank says, again bringing his needy friends into this. "But now remember, her life might not be as easy or perfect as you think it is."

"Yeah right, Frank!" I laugh. "It'll be tough to decide which of Marina's seventy swimsuits to wear and petting that adorable dolphin and getting a tan all day!"

"Well, anyway..." Frank just shakes his head like he doesn't realize that I've got this one. Piece of cake. "Pay attention 'cause those MMBs might have a thing or two to teach you about this little swim team snafu," Frank explains, but I'm not really listening to him anymore.

"Uh-huh," I mumble.

"Alrighty then." Frank looks at me a little sideways and then jumps up and leans toward me in the mirror. "And don't forget your trusty genie pocket mirror in the drawer there...I'm guessing there aren't a lot of mirrors on Flynn Tide's boat."

"Right! Good thinking, Frank! TTYL!" I say, thinking there's no way he'll get that.

"OK!" Frank yells back, changing from a clear picture in my mirror to a watery blob. "TTFN!"

I kind of love that genie.

* * *

Not to be full of myself or anything, but I'm kind of getting to be an MMB professional. Last night I laid out my clothes and set my alarm to go off extra early today. (I picked 4:44, because I love it when numbers repeat. On regular school days I always set it for 5:55, even though I don't technically have to be up until 6:15. I'm sort of strange like that.) The alarm blares and I bolt straight up in bed. *It's showtime, folks!*

I tiptoe into the bathroom to brush my teeth, then I put on my favorite track suit, the hot pink one with white stripes down the sides. Even though I won't be wearing it when I wake up as Marina, I feel sporty when I wear it so it seemed fitting. Plus it has pockets so I have somewhere to stash my genie pocket mirror. I slip the mirror in the side pocket and zip it up nice and tight. After giving my hair a quick scrunching—there's no sense trying to *comb* it or anything, since I'm sure it'll be wet in like five minutes—I walk over to my closet and pull down the MMBs from the tippy-top shelf. They smell like chicken curry mixed with burnt marshmallows. Don't ask me why, but they do.

I pull on the MMBs and stand up tall. Then I walk over to my mirror. I've got to tell you, beat-up old cowboy boots look pretty funny with my track suit, but I won't be wearing this crazy getup for long. "With these MMBs I choose," I say to my reflection, "a day in Marina Tide's shoes!"

About the Authors

Jenna McCarthy is a writer, speaker, and aspiring drummer who has wanted magical boots since she learned to walk. She lives with her husband, daughters, cats, and dogs in sunny Southern California.

Carolyn Evans is an author, speaker, and singer/songwriter who once opened for Pat Benatar—you can ask your mom who that is. She loves traveling to faraway places but is just as happy at home with her husband and kids, living by a river in South Carolina and dreaming up grand adventures for Maggie Malone.

The Cupcake Club

A treasure trove of delicious treats—the Cupcake Club will satisfy any sweet tooth! Catch up on the first five books in this popular new series by New York Times bestselling author Sheryl Berk and her cupcake-loving daughter, Carrie. Each book features yummy original recipes from the story and fun extras to enjoy!